"What scares you about North Vietnam?" Gerber whispered

"It truly is my home," Kit answered. "If we are caught, I will be shot as a spy, but not before I am tortured. They have some people who enjoy that work..."

"Kit, if any of us are caught, we're going to be shot as spies."

"Please, do not let them catch me." Her voice was insistent, with a note of terror.

"I can't—"

"You *can*," she interrupted. "You can make sure that I am not captured. Please, Captain. As a friend you cannot deny me this one request."

Gerber sat back, forcing himself into the corner between the side of the truck and the cab. With his free hand he wiped the sweat from his face. He needed a breath of fresh air. He felt hot and his stomach was fluttering because he knew what Kit was asking of him.

If they got into a situation where they might be captured, she wanted him to kill her.

"Vietnam: Ground Zero... are books to linger in the mind long after their reading."
—*The Midwest Book Review*

VIETNAM: GROUND ZERO
GUIDELINES

ERIC HELM

A GOLD EAGLE BOOK FROM
WORLDWIDE

TORONTO · NEW YORK · LONDON · PARIS
AMSTERDAM · STOCKHOLM · HAMBURG
ATHENS · MILAN · TOKYO · SYDNEY

First edition October 1987

ISBN 0-373-62708-4

Printed in Canada

VIETNAM: GROUND ZERO

GUIDELINES

ERIC HELM

PROLOGUE

OVER THE GULF OF TONKIN

The darkened coast of North Vietnam, painted in a glowing green line on the F-4 Phantom fighter-bomber's radarscope, was still almost a hundred miles distant. Captain David Bidwell, a lean young man, kept his face pressed close to the blackout hood, his eyes glued to the screen with its sweeping green arm, studying the coastline, searching for the point where they were supposed to cross it. A necessary task for their rendezvous with the Wild Weasel escort.

The pilot, Captain Richard Wornell, a shorter, stockier man than his WSO, began a long slow descent that would bring them closer to the ground. He kept his gaze outside of the cockpit, looking down at the silvery wisps of the cloud deck, which was lighted by the nearly full moon above them. Over his shoulder, the stars blazed like thousands of pin-sized spotlights in the night sky. To his right was the dark shape of another aircraft.

Without a word to either his backseater or his wingman, he began a gradual turn, following the VDI, which had slipped slightly to the left. As the wingman pulled away, they entered the overcast. Wornell now could see nothing other than the blackness around him, broken by flashes of gray from the cloud cover and the dull glow of the red and green navigation lights of the other aircraft.

Bidwell knew exactly where they were. The radar mapped the coast with unerring accuracy. He sat straight up for a moment, his eyes now on the other instruments as he arched his back to relax the muscles. Then he pressed his face to the hood as the coast of North Vietnam slipped under their aircraft. Bidwell told Wornell that they were no longer feet wet.

They broke out of the clouds and continued their descent until they were close to the deck. Wornell squeezed the control yoke until his hand ached, but he couldn't relax. He was nervous, flying at nearly five hundred knots, at night, so close to the ground.

To the right he saw a stream of tracers streaking upward, looking like a string of glowing green baseballs. Moments later a second string was fired, but neither burst was near him nor his wingman. Probably just a North Vietnamese farmer shooting at the roar of the jet engines with his militia issued AK-47.

They raced on, climbing to avoid hills, then dropping back into the valleys. Wornell, moving his head as if on a swivel, ignored his instruments now because he was much too close to the ground. Their response was too slow at this altitude, and he didn't have the time to glance at them, and instead tried to concentrate on the roar of his own twin turbines, waiting for a change in the pitch that would warn him of impending disaster.

There was a buzz in Wornell's headset and the sky around him burst into flame as a 57 mm antiaircraft gun opened fire. Wornell ignored the flashes, tightening his grip on the yoke. His wingman, for a moment nothing more than a shadow in the distance, moved nearer and then fell away.

"Got a SAM low light," said Bidwell.

"Weasel Lead, this is Baron Lead," radioed Wornell. "We have a SAM warning."

"Baron, this is Weasel Lead. We have a radar lock. Going in," came the reply.

"Radar's off," said Bidwell.

Wornell grinned at that. If the North Vietnamese operators didn't keep the acquisition and tracking radars on, they couldn't fire the missiles. And if they did fire, the missiles would be ineffective as they blindly climbed into the dark. They needed the radar guidance.

"More Triple A," said Bidwell.

Wornell glanced to the right. It was as if the ground was carpeted with strobes. The muzzle flashes of the weapons sparkled, sending up fountains of green tracers. The sky was alive with them, swarming upward, trying to knock down the American aircraft.

"Got visual on a SAM Two site," said Bidwell.

Wornell saw the missile site, a rosebud pattern on the ground, the black ribbons of road leading to the missile launch areas. There were revetments of dirt around each missile, making it difficult for bombers to take out all six positions at once. Hidden away were the radar vans, the maintenance trucks and repair vehicles and the command post.

The site was dark and Wornell saw no one on it as they flew by. The radar vans and command posts that were usually targets of the Wild Weasels, were somewhere else, separated from the actual launch complex by as much as a klick.

As they crossed the complex, Wornell relaxed slightly. There were still no warning lights on his panel. The missile radars, the Spoon Rest and the Fan Song, which were needed to acquire the target and guide the missiles, had been shut down. The Weasels had done their jobs.

Then out of the corner of his eye Wornell saw a flash as rocket motors ignited. Before he could react, the missile was off the ground. Helplessly he watched the streak of yellow-white flame homing on the tail of his wingman. An explosion at the rear of the Phantom seemed to lift it up and flip it over. A ball of red-orange flame burst around the aircraft, enveloping it completely. Then there was a secondary explosion followed by a shower of flaming debris raining onto the rice paddies of North Vietnam.

"Jesus H. Christ on a crutch," said Bidwell. "What in the fuck hit him?"

"Missile," said Wornell. The single word nearly stuck in his throat.

"There were no warning lights."

Wornell keyed the mike for the radio. "We're taking missile fire down here."

"Roger," came the reply from Weasel Lead. "We have no warning lights."

"Baron Two is down to missile fire," said Wornell. There was no emotion in his voice. He was merely reporting a fact to the Weasel Lead.

"There's one coming at us," yelled Bidwell.

"Hit the chaff," ordered Wornell as he rolled the jet to the left, diving toward the ground. An instant later he hauled back on the yoke, beginning a spiraling climb that rocked both men, slamming them against the restraining straps of their shoulder harnesses.

"Chaff's no good," said Bidwell.

Wornell rolled the aircraft to the left and then back to the right, finally diving toward the ground again, pulling up at the last moment as the engines screamed and the aircraft shuddered, fighting the stress. As he broke to the left the missile slammed harmlessly into a rice paddy.

"Another one!" said Bidwell. "Where the fuck are they coming from?"

Wornell had no chance to answer. He began a steep climb, rolled the aircraft over into a power dive, twisting back and forth. He couldn't check to see the missile's progress. All he could do was flip from one maneuver to another in an attempt to evade the missile, using its greater speed, which produced a wider turning radius, against it.

As he leveled out, he was smashed forward, as if someone had struck the back of his seat with a sledgehammer. He could feel pain in his shoulders and a curtain of black descended until his vision was like looking down a long, dark tunnel. Around him he was aware of buzzers and bells and the cockpit seemed to be filled with smoke. There was a whining, two-tone warning buzzer demanding attention.

For a moment he couldn't figure out what had happened. The aircraft was buffeting, bouncing around like a speeding car on a rutted road. Glancing out, he noticed that the wings were riddled by shrapnel and trailing a thin plume of smoke.

Wornell tried to initiate a climb. The nose of the aircraft came up, but the shuddering became worse as the jet threatened to tear itself apart. Before Wornell could order the bailout, the canopy was ripped away and the cockpit was filled with the roar of the wind.

Seconds later Wornell ejected, his arms wrapped about his head to protect it. The wall of wind hit him like a brick through a plate-glass window and forced his arms against his helmet. Clear of the burning aircraft, he opened his eyes as the jet began a long, shallow descent into the rice paddies below. A spectacular yellow-orange explosion lit up the night sky as the plane struck the ground, destroying itself in a roiling cloud of black smoke.

The parachute popped, jerking at Wornell. Not far away, the backseater was hanging from his own canopy, drifting down into the night, sliding away from Wornell until he lost sight of the man in the darkness. A single stream of tracers reached out of the dark, arcing toward him, but didn't come close. He couldn't hear the sound of the firing or see the muzzle flashes of the weapon.

Wornell landed with a splash in a foul-smelling rice paddy. He rolled to his right and hit the quick release, dropping his chute away from him. Wet from head to foot, he scrambled to his feet, then rubbed a hand over his face, trying to wipe the excrement-laden water from his eyes. After his vision returned to normal, he reached to his right and drew the .38-caliber revolver from the holster sewn into his survival vest. Slowly he turned three hundred and sixty degrees to survey his surroundings.

The world around him was so quiet that he wondered if he had lost his hearing during the bailout. After a moment or two he became aware of the distant pop of Triple A as the tracers danced skyward. Myriad streams crisscrossed each other like a cheap fireworks display.

Knee deep in the clammy paddy, and with water dripping from the barrel of his weapon, he gazed at the flash and pop of flack as the enemy gunners tried to down more of the American planes. The breath was rasping in his throat, as if he had run a long distance, and he found that he was suddenly quite thirsty. His desire for water nearly overwhelmed him.

Out loud, he said, "It's not fair. We didn't get a launch warning. They can't do that."

1

UBON AIR FORCE BASE
THAILAND

The special meeting had been called for thirteen hundred hours on Thursday, the twenty-fourth. Jerry Maxwell, dressed in a rumpled white suit, stood in the hot tropical sun, sweating heavily. Maxwell was a short man who had lost weight during his tour in Vietnam so that he looked gaunt. His black hair was sweat damp and plastered against his forehead. Dark circles under his light-colored eyes contrasted sharply with his permanently sunburned skin, and the fact that he needed a shave all helped to give him the appearance of a starving clown. He watched the F-4 Phantoms taxiing toward the runways in front of him. The sleek aircraft were camouflage painted and carrying heavy bomb payloads, taking off for missions against suspected enemy positions in South Vietnam, Cambodia and southern Laos.

Maxwell turned, squinted at the palm tree near the door to Operations, and then stepped back into the shade. He drew a handkerchief from his hip pocket and mopped his face, leaving a light brown stain on the cloth. A Jeep with three passengers pulled into the parking space in front of the Operations hangar. Two of the vehicle's occupants were dressed in crisp, starched jungle fatigues topped off by soft baseball caps, and carried M-16s. The other was bareheaded and wore a lightweight, light blue suit, looking as if he couldn't wait to get inside where there was some air-conditioning.

As they hopped out of the vehicle, the man in the suit approached Maxwell and said, "Come on, Jerry. No need to stand around out here sweating."

"Yes, sir." The group moved toward the door and entered the building, running smack into a wall of cold air.

They made their way down a narrow corridor, which was paneled in dark wood about halfway up and then painted a light blue to the ceiling. The floor was waxed concrete, and an unbroken line of fluorescent lights ran along the middle of the ceiling. They took the first stairwell they came to and climbed to the second floor. Not far away was a doorway leading to a conference room.

It was typical of the conference rooms on any American military base. In the center of the room sat a large table. On it was a water pitcher beaded with moisture and surrounded by six glasses. There were a dozen metal chairs around the table, with a high-backed leather one at its head. A bank of windows, partially hidden behind venetian blinds, looked out onto the airfield. On the other three walls were watercolors of jets in revetments, taking off, dropping bombs, shooting down MiGs, and limping home.

Maxwell slipped into one of the chairs and shivered as the cold air dried the sweat on his body. He reached for one of the glasses, decided that he didn't really want a drink, and rocked back, waiting. Within minutes they were joined by four more military officers and two civilians.

One of the officers was an Air Force brigadier general. He wore tailored jungle fatigues with embroidered stars on the collar and command pilot wings above the left breast.

He moved toward the leather chair at the head of the table, but instead of sitting, he stood behind it, and placed his hands on the back rest as he surveyed the men around him.

"Gentlemen," he began. "For those of you who don't know me, I'm General Thomas Christie and I'll be chairing this meeting. Our recommendations will be forwarded through the chain of command to both the Pentagon and General Westmoreland. With me are Colonel Edward Kent, Majors Andrew Dillon, Roger Quinn and the Wild Weasel flight leader, Terry McMance. Next to him is Captain Charles Fallon."

Christie then sat down and looked at the civilians. "Mr. Cornett, would you be so kind as to introduce your people?"

Cornett, a short, stocky man sporting a beard that was inconsistent with the clean-shaven ravings of most of the power structure nodded and said, "Certainly, General. To my right are Tim Underwood, Paul Harris and Jerry Maxwell."

"Thank you," said Christie. He picked up a black folder with the Air Force crest embossed on the cover and opened it. "I have a simple agenda for the meeting and would like to stick to it as closely as possible. If anyone has any objections, we'll discuss those in a few moments."

He glanced at the men around him and said, "All right. First we'll get a report from Major McMance concerning his observations over North Vietnam two nights ago. Captain Fallon will supplement that description with his own observations. Colonel Kent will discuss the recent developments of the Soviet SAM force."

Cornett interrupted at that point. "Mr. Underwood has made a recent study of the Soviet SAM threat and might have some insights along those lines. That includes developments of new missile systems that are not deployed outside the Soviet Union. We do have some photographic intelligence available to us."

"Good," said Christie. "Finally, Major Quinn and Major Dillon will discuss the possible tactics we can use to counter this new threat." He looked up from his notes. "That about cover it?"

There was a murmur of agreement and then silence. Christie smiled, "From this point, I think everything we say will be classified as secret. I don't want any of it discussed outside of this room."

When no one said anything, Christie nodded. "Okay, Major McMance, you want to lead off?"

"Yes, sir." McMance stood and moved so that he was near the head of the table. McMance was a tall, thin man with black hair and bushy eyebrows. His face was tanned a deep brown and with his brown eyes, he looked Latin.

"Is everyone familiar with the Wild Weasel concept?" He glanced from man to man and saw a couple of them shaking their heads.

"The short course, then," he said, grinning. "The idea is simple enough. The North Vietnamese, using equipment supplied by the Soviets, are shooting at our bombing forces. Almost all the acquisition and guidance is radar controlled, whether for the SAMs or the Triple A. The Wild Weasels detect the radar signals and, using Shrike missiles that ride the radar beams back to their sources, attack the radar vans and the co-located command vehicles. Knocking out the radar effectively blinds the antiaircraft capability whether it is missile or ZSU-23, S-60 or 57 mm."

"But the missiles themselves are not damaged?" queried Underwood.

"No, sir. The command vehicles and radar vans are normally a couple of klicks from the missile or Triple A site."

"Then the missiles can still be fired," said Underwood.

"Yes, sir. The Triple A also has the capability to be fired through optical sights, but it becomes very ineffective that way. Most of the missiles won't be fired because of the lack of tracking radar."

"What if they simply turn off the radar while you're overhead?" The puzzled look that Underwood wore began to disappear.

"That's the beauty of the system," replied McMance, smiling. "If the radar set is off, they can't detect and track our planes. If they turn it on, we attack it. Either way, we've won."

McMance hesitated and then looked at Christie.

"If no one has any further questions," said the general, "we'll move on."

"I've seen no figures on how effective this Wild Weasel thing has been," said Underwood.

McMance had started back to his seat, but halted. "After implementation of the concept, our losses to enemy antiaircraft dropped off significantly. Prior to that, losses were running so high that it was becoming suicidal to attack the North."

"Captain Fallon," said Christie, "do you want to tell us what happened two days ago."

"Yes, sir." Fallon stood, but didn't move away from his seat. Like McMance, he was tall and thin. Reduced body weight of the pilots and electronic warfare officers meant higher payloads. His hair was sandy blond and his face burned pink. He had light, washed-out eyes.

Fallon's voice was high and squeaky. He cleared his throat once and said, "The thing that bothers us is that there were missile launches from a standard SA-2 site, but no radar indications that we were being tracked. No indications that the site was active."

"My information," said Underwood, "is that the Soviets are moving the radars and command vehicles off the sites. You wouldn't get the radar detection indications if the radar vans have been moved."

"I understand that, sir," said Fallon. "We've seen the North Vietnamese following that example. We just flood the whole area with aircraft and hit them when we get the radar detection. Besides, the jets being painted would get SAM lights. No, sir, we believe there has been a drastic change in the Soviet missile technology."

Underwood emitted a laugh that sounded like a bark. "That's quite a conclusion based on a single raid."

"We saw launches off a SAM Two site and there were no radar indications. If they can do it again, we'll have no defense against it. Their Triple A, designed to fire up to fifteen, twenty thousand feet and to use optical as well as radar sights, coupled to the Guideline with a range of up to ninety thousand feet will create a protective umbrella that we can't penetrate. We can't fly under it or over it. The air war suddenly evaporates."

"You're being overly dramatic," said Underwood.

Christie slammed a hand to the tabletop. "Damn it! You don't have to fly those missions, Underwood. You have no idea what it's like flying into a wall of flack and missiles. If we can't counter this threat, you're going to see a reduction in the air war."

Underwood stared at the general for a moment and then looked to Cornett. "Sir, I think this is an overreaction to a perceived new threat. I don't think we have a problem here except one created by the Air Force."

Cornett nodded his agreement and said, "General?"

Christie turned his attention to Fallon. "Captain, can you make your case clearer for these men?"

"Yes, sir. Up until two nights ago, we had no launches from a Guideline SAM site without a radar indication. Now that indication may have been fleeting. The operator turning on his radar, getting a blip and turning it right back off. No matter, because we picked up the warning indications. Two nights ago, we got no radar indications, but we did get missile launches from those sites."

"Does that make it clear, Underwood?" asked Christie.

"No, sir, it doesn't."

"Damn it, man," snapped Cornett. "It means they've developed a new guidance system for their missiles and we have to come up with a way to counter it."

Underwood nodded, his eyes on the table. He looked like a little boy who had been reprimanded in school. All he said was, "Oh."

"Yes, oh," said Cornett. "Now, are we certain that the launches came from an SA-2?"

"From the site, yes," said Fallon. "There is no question about it."

For the next hour they discussed the state of Soviet missile technology. The CIA representatives argued against a sudden improvement in the Soviets' missile abilities and then pointed out that even if there had been one, it wouldn't be given to the North Vietnamese.

Maxwell listened to it all calmly, never speaking. When they all wound down, he said, "I'd like to add one thing. In May, 1960, Soviet missile technology took a giant leap forward when they knocked down a U-2. Totally unexpected. And not unlike the situation we find ourselves in now."

"Except the Soviets didn't give that technology to an ally," said Underwood.

Maxwell ignored Underwood, looked at the general. "He's right about it. They didn't give it away, but they did use it to knock down the U-2, which told us something that we didn't know. That they could do it. We have the same situation here. A sudden improvement in their technology."

"Then you see nothing inconsistent with their behavior in the past," said Christie.

"No, sir. I think we'd better investigate this further as quickly as possible."

Christie closed his folder. "Gentlemen, I think we've gone far enough for today. We'll meet again tomorrow. At that time I'll want recommendations to take up the chain of command."

Outside, as they walked to their Jeeps, Cornett pulled Maxwell to the side. He glanced right and left to make sure that no one was near him. Then he pulled off his sunglasses and stared straight into Maxwell's eyes.

"Jerry," he said, and then stopped as the scream of a plane taking off drowned out everything he said. When it was airborne, he continued. "I want you to return to Saigon tonight. We're not going to need you here for the rest of this."

"I didn't contribute much to it today," agreed Maxwell.

"You weren't ordered here to contribute to this discussion. I wanted you to listen in. I did that because you've been working with the Special Forces SOG in Saigon, and those guys always have answers."

"Yes, sir."

"Then you can see where I'm going with this. Hell, we can't put a CIA man into the North to look things over. He'd stick out like a sore thumb. And we don't have anyone infiltrated into the Soviet delegation there. Besides we've no one trained to operate in the jungle..."

"You want me to come up with someone to go into the North and look at one of these missile sites."

"Yes. You've got the people to do it. Some of those Sneaky Petes you work with would be perfect. Have them parachute in, take a look at one of the sites, steal a fucking guidance system if they have to, and then bug out. Answers everyone's questions and gives us all the information we need to counter the threat."

"I don't know about this," said Maxwell.

Again Cornett looked around, as if afraid that someone was going to sneak up to listen. He wiped the perspiration from his forehead and slipped his sunglasses on. "Don't bullshit me, Jerry. You've had people in the North before. Or if you haven't, SOG has. They've been operating there for years. That's not a problem and you know it."

"No," said Maxwell shaking his head. "No, I guess it isn't."

"Okay," said Cornett. "What I want you to do is catch the first ride back to Saigon and set something up. I want those men on the ground in North Vietnam inside of forty-eight hours."

Now Maxwell laughed. "I can't put something like that together that fast. The coordination, getting the men together and then into the field is impossible that quickly. Hell, it'll take a week to work out the airlift."

"Jerry, you have your orders. I want an answer to this inside the week. We don't have time to fuck around on it. I know that the President will be asking the DCI for some answers and I don't want him to have to say that he doesn't know. I want him to be able to hand the President a completed report on this so that he'll see we have it wired."

Maxwell rubbed a hand through his hair. He looked at the ground and then up at a nearby palm. The sound of the jets on the airfield threatened to drown out their voices. The light breeze was more like the wind from a blast furnace.

"I'll do what I can," Maxwell said. "I can put a team in there, I just don't know if forty-eight hours is enough time."

"You can have whatever you need except extra time. Priorities will be arranged all the way. If you run into trouble, you call me and I'll see to it that the roadblock disappears."

"Yes, sir. I'll get right on it."

"And Jerry," said Cornett, "we have to keep this discreet. The political situation in the States is volatile. We don't want a lot of publicity on this."

"I understand," said Maxwell. It was the same kind of directive that he worked under all the time.

2

MICHELIN RUBBER PLANTATION NORTHWEST OF SAIGON RVN

U.S. Army Special Forces Master Sergeant Anthony B. Fetterman stood in the shade of the rubber trees, one hand on the rough bark, and watched the ARVN ranger trainees sweep through the bunkerline.

Fetterman was a diminutive man with black, balding hair, dark, cold, hard eyes and a heritage that he claimed to be Aztec. The two hundred would-be graduates of the ARVN ranger school were having their final examination in the field with the American Special Forces.

There had been reports of VC operating in the vicinity of Dau Tieng. The Saigon government wanted the ARVN, with the help of the Special Forces, to search for enemy activity.

Fetterman was out there, as was Captain MacKenzie K. Gerber, to evaluate the unit and to coordinate assistance if the rangers happened to find more of the enemy than they expected. He waited as three men explored a bunker, two standing outside it, on either side of the entrance, while the third man dived into it. When the man reappeared, shaking his head, Fetterman relaxed and moved toward the Special Forces captain, checking his watch.

"I make it two more hours," said Fetterman. He wiped the sweat on his face with his sleeve.

Gerber nodded but didn't speak. He was a career officer, and on the promotion list for major. Gerber was a tall, well-muscled man with brown hair and blue eyes. At the moment he looked hot and miserable, the sweat turning his jungle fatigues black under the arms and down the back. He held his M-16 by the rear sight mount, which looked like a luggage handle. At first his attention was on Fetterman and then he glanced at the ARVN rangers as they filtered through the rubber trees.

Unlike the jungle and forests that surrounded the plantation, this was a well-manicured area that looked like an overgrown orchard. The trees were evenly spaced, planted in rows with a thin ground cover. It was almost like a park inside the plantation.

Finally he said, "Let's get them out of here and move toward the west and the base there."

"Yes, sir," Fetterman said. Resignedly he turned and stepped closer to the Vietnamese officer who had attached himself to the RTO. Fetterman had cautioned the man three times that the enemy liked to shoot the people with the radio man, figuring they'd get the officers, but the ARVN wouldn't listen.

Almost as if to prove his point, a single shot rang out in the distance. There was a muffled pop and a snap as the round passed overhead. Fetterman dived to the right, twisting around, looking for the source. A number of the men were standing upright as if they hadn't figured out what was going on. One of them was pointing to the north.

"Hit the dirt!" Fetterman shouted.

There was a second shot and a scream of pain. One of the rangers grabbed his shoulder as he fell to the ground. He spun, rocking from side to side, his right hand against his left shoulder. Blood was welling between his fingers as he continued to scream.

A ripple of firing broke out, the rattling of M-16 rifles. The men had scattered, taking up positions behind the trees, along the sides of the bunkers, or on the ground with nothing between them and the enemy. Some of them fired their weapon by holding it around the trunk of the tree and squeezing the trigger without looking for a target.

Fetterman crawled to his left, where the wounded man was still screaming. He grabbed the man and held him down. With his free hand, he peeled the ARVN's fingers from the wound. It was a clean shot through the shoulder, and the blood was washing it. Fetterman shook out a bandage from his first-aid kit and pressed it to the wound and then let the man grab it again, holding the gauze in place.

In the meantime, Gerber had worked his way to the RTO and the ARVN ranger commander. The ARVN CO was crouched behind a bunker, his hands holding his helmet tightly to his head. Although he couldn't see the man's face, Gerber was certain that he had his eyes closed.

"Dai uy," Gerber said. "You'd better organize your response. You have a sniper, two men at most out there."

"We shoot and they run," the CO said without looking up. He remained frozen in place.

"They won't run away. They'll wait and then shoot someone else the first chance they get."

"We shoot and they run," he repeated.

"Dai uy," said Gerber. "It's your responsibility to get the men up and moving."

This time the man didn't speak. Gerber stared at him for a moment. Around him the Vietnamese were still shooting in ill coordinated and ragged volleys. Bullets were snapping through the thick green leaves of the rubber trees, and slamming into the trunks.

Off to the right, one of the Vietnamese NCOs was suddenly on his feet. Shouting at his men, he pointed deeper into the trees. He ran to one man, jerked him to his feet and shoved him toward the enemy position.

Gerber took a final look at the officer who hadn't moved or spoken since the last fusillade, then leaped up. He raced toward the Vietnamese sergeant and dropped to the ground near him. Gerber wasn't going to say a word to him, unless he did something stupid.

The NCO ran to another of the Vietnamese and snatched the M-79 grenade launcher out of his hands. He screamed at the soldier who then surrendered the spare ammo for the weapon. The man refused to get to his feet.

Gerber shook his head and mumbled, ''This is the best they've got?''

The NCO was up and moving from one tree to the next. He stopped, shouted a command. The firing, which had been tapering off, suddenly started up again. A couple of the soldiers pointed their weapons at the sky and pulled the triggers, firing on full auto until the bolts locked back, their rifles empty.

Others were shooting into the trees, firing short bursts and reloading as necessary. The Vietnamese NCO began to move again, dodging from tree to tree. Leaping to cover, he rolled right, and then clawed his way forward.

Gerber followed him, watching his every move. He was grinning, thinking of Captain Minh, the camp commander when Gerber had been assigned to Camp A-555 on his first tour. Minh had been the same kind of self-starter. A soldier's soldier in anyone's army. There were so few of them that it was a pleasure to find one.

The NCO slid into a depression, broke open the M-79 and dropped a round into it. He flipped up the sight, worked it up and down and then sighted on where he suspected the enemy sniper was hiding. He pulled the trigger and waited to see where the round hit. He ducked, his eyes on the enemy position. There was a dull thump and a tiny cloud of black smoke at the base of a tree.

As the NCO fired two more times, Gerber ran toward the wounded man. Fetterman had dragged him to cover behind one of the trees and had dressed the wound. He now held his canteen to the man's lips, letting him drink.

"How bad?" asked Gerber.

"Through and through. I think the shoulder is pretty torn up, but he's not in danger of dying right now."

"Medevac?"

"I'm not thrilled with that idea, Captain. It could be a trap to get us to bring in a chopper and give someone else a shot at it. Could be what they had in mind."

"Yeah," said Gerber. "Get the Vietnamese medic on this guy and then you get a sweep going to the west, toward the LZ there. I'll be checking on that NCO. See what he does next."

Fetterman grinned. "Since these guys are still in school, I say they flunk."

Gerber turned and ran back, dodging around the rubber trees. He dropped to the ground behind the NCO, who had stopped firing his M-79 and was watching the field in front of him. There was the pop and crack of weapons as the troops fired single shots now. A few of the Vietnamese fired tracers, bright burning rubies that bounced across the ground. None of the fire was incoming.

Finally the NCO got to his feet, jogged to the right and fell next to a man with an M-16. The sergeant took the rifle, leaving the soldier with the grenade launcher and spare ammo. Then, on his feet again, he pointed to several men, gesturing that they should move forward. Together, the line of infantry advanced, half of them covering, while the others sprinted among the trees. When the forward line had moved twenty or thirty yards, they fell into firing positions so that the men behind could move up.

They continued that maneuver for a couple of minutes. Gerber followed behind the rear guard, watching them carefully, but offered no advice or help. As he approached there was a burst of rifle fire. A single staccato ripping of M-16 ammo followed it. Everyone dived for cover and shooting broke out along the line.

The Vietnamese NCO was on his feet suddenly, shouting at his men. He ran forward, hurdled a small bush and disappeared behind it. A second later there was a long burst from an M-16, two return shots from an AK-47 and then complete silence. The sergeant suddenly reappeared, the AK held over his head like a trophy.

The Vietnamese rangers lost the little discipline they had. A dozen of them leaped to their feet, running forward toward the sergeant. They were screaming wildly, like rebel soldiers storming the Yankee lines. Gerber followed, yelling at them to watch their security, watch for booby traps, but no one was listening.

From the trees came a shot, followed by four more, all from M-16s. Gerber arrived in time to see two of the Vietnamese rangers firing their weapons into the heads of the dead sniper and his spotter, splattering their blood and brains over the soft decaying ground.

"Cease fire!" ordered Gerber. He snapped his fingers at the NCO who was standing off to the side.

One of the rangers looked at Gerber, the anger on his face unmistakable. Then, in defiance, he spun and put a burst into one of the dead VC's chests. The impact of the rounds caused the body to shudder. Blood had stained his shirt a rusty brown and soaked the ground around him. One of the bullets opened the abdomen, spilling his guts to the earth. The odor of the bowels drifted on the light breeze.

"Knock it off," snapped Gerber. "You might need that ammo later. Don't waste it."

The Vietnamese sergeant who had taken charge said something and then stepped next to the shooting man. He grabbed at the weapon, pushing it aside. Then he slapped the man twice. For a moment it looked as if the man was going to shoot the sergeant. Then he turned and stomped away.

"I get them," the sergeant told Gerber.

"Thank you, Sergeant. Very well done." Gerber glanced at the bodies and then at the man's name tape. Le Duc. "Now, is there something else to be done?"

"Oh, yes, sir. I check bodies for papers and insignia. We find out good things from papers and insignia. That helps us to find more VC to kill."

Gerber couldn't help grinning. Trying to teach the Vietnamese how to fight the war was a futile effort. They couldn't understand that a live prisoner was more valuable than a dead man. They couldn't understand why they should collect papers and insignia and not ears and fingers. But once in a while you came across a Vietnamese who seemed to understand exactly what was happening. Someone who was willing to listen and to learn. Sergeant Le Duc was one of the few who did.

"Get the weapons and anything else you can and then return to the group."

"Yes, sir."

Gerber returned to find Fetterman had gotten a perimeter established with the help of the captain who had finally decided to move. It was a ragged perimeter that wouldn't have lasted long if the enemy decided to attack them. The men were scattered through the trees, facing away from the center, each man with a friend close at hand.

"How's the wounded man?"

"Sooner we get him out of here, the better off we're going to be."

"Got the sniper and his spotter," said Gerber. "Doesn't seem to be anyone else with them."

"But there was a lot of shooting over there."

"Yeah. The Viets riddled the bodies when they found them." Gerber crouched, fingered his canteen but decided against taking a drink. "Let's get the sweep under way and secure the LZ. We'll get a Medevac in here and then a flight to take us out."

"You think the exercise is over?" asked Fetterman.

"Tony, these guys are terrible. They haven't the slightest idea of what's going on. I think some district chief designated them rangers to get some equipment for them. Then, because the chief had influence, no one wanted to irritate them with training. We get into a fight with them and they're going to all get killed."

"Yes, sir," said Fetterman. "I noticed their noise discipline was lax and they didn't have much unit integrity. Not to mention that the leadership by the officers didn't exist. What are you going to do?"

"Write a report and give it to the ARVN command and Saigon so they can file it."

"And then?"

"See if I can't con SOG or Maxwell or MACV into letting me go up to Bromhead's camp for a couple of weeks on a fact-finding tour so that I can hide out while the ARVN command cools down."

"What facts will you be looking for?"

"I don't know. There must be something going on that we don't know about. Maybe follow up on the reports of VC and NVA infiltrating the area in unprecedented numbers."

"Yes, sir." Fetterman got to his feet. "Why don't I get these people moving so we can get the fuck out of the heat?"

"Good plan."

THREE HOURS LATER, Gerber, now in clean jungle fatigues and having showered and shaved, sat in the open air bar of the Carasel Hotel in downtown Saigon.

Within minutes, after Fetterman had ordered the evacuation of the wounded man and then called for the helicopters to take them all out, the dustoff chopper had come and gone, and a flight of Hueys had diverted to pick up the rangers. From their camp at Trung Lap, it had been no trouble to hop a ride to Tan Son Nhut. When they had returned to Saigon, they had taken a Jeep from Tan Son Nhut into the city where they had rooms at the Carasel.

The bar where Gerber sat was eight or ten feet above the street. It was a concrete balcony loaded with tropical plants and ferns that obscured some of the view. A bar constructed from stone and red leather and plastic stood at one end, with a single bartender working there. Several Vietnamese women, wearing skimpy costumes, roamed among the closely packed tables, serving the customers, mostly civilians from the embassy or the news media.

Gerber's table sat in the shadow of a nearby building, a spot carefully chosen so that the late afternoon breeze would dry the sweat from his forehead and face. He sipped the ice cold beer, delivered by the sweating barmaid and thought about the nature of the war.

When Fetterman, now wearing a fresh uniform that didn't show any signs of the muggy afternoon, appeared and sat down, Gerber said, "I think I know what's wrong with the Vietnam war."

Fetterman raised an eyebrow, took a sip of the beer that Gerber had ordered for him. "What's that, Captain?"

"Simply that there is no incentive to end it. None whatsoever."

"Yes, sir," said Fetterman. He set the beer on the table, glancing at a group of civilians who were laughing and shouting. "No incentive," he repeated.

"You see," continued Gerber, leaning back in his chair and lacing his fingers behind his head, "a couple of hours ago we were in the field, hot and miserable, sweating and thirsty. Now we sit in a bar, still hot, but we could be cool if we went inside, sipping beer and looking at the ladies. And if we wanted, we could retire to our rooms, watch TV, order room service, and just relax in the air-conditioning until tomorrow."

"And since we're no longer uncomfortable," said Fetterman, "we have no incentive to end the war."

"Right. Now in World War Two, the soldier was in for the duration. Granted, from the landings in France to the end of the war in Europe was something like eleven months, but the soldier who landed in France might have been fighting in Italy before that, or North Africa. They were uncomfortable and miserable and knew they had to stay until they ended the war. They didn't know how long that would be."

"So you're saying," said Fetterman, "that the year-long tour doesn't provide an incentive to end the war."

"Not only that," answered Gerber, "but look at our surroundings. Not exactly uncomfortable. We spend a day or two in the field and then we're back here in our air-conditioned rooms, watching TV and chasing women."

"There are men in the field," said Fetterman. "Men who stay out there most of the time."

"True enough," said Gerber, "but they're the exception rather than the rule. Hell, Tony, how many guys are in Vietnam now? Four, five hundred thousand? And of those how many end up in a combat environment. One in eight? One in nine? And even those guys know they've only got to survive eleven, twelve months and they're out of it. All the officers are rotated every six months. What's the point in knocking yourself out if you know you'll be free and clear in less than a year?"

Fetterman nodded without comment and sipped his beer. He had heard all this before. It seemed that lately, every time they had come back from the field and sat around drinking beer, the captain got off on his this-is-what's-wrong-with-the-war speech. That was not to say that Gerber wasn't right about it.

Smiling, Fetterman said, "If you'd like, sir, I'm sure we could volunteer for a mission that would get us into the field for a few weeks. We could sweat all day humping through the jungle, be miserable all night sleeping in trees and waiting for the sniper's bullet or ambush to cut us down. No TV or air-conditioning or room service."

"That's not what I mean and you know it," snapped Gerber. Then realizing that he had said it all before, he grinned. "Actually, the real solution for this is to call up the National Guard. Those guys would end it in a weekend so they could go home."

At that moment a group of journalists burst into the bar, shouting at the waitress for instant service, hailing at other news people already there, and demanding that the music be turned up so they could hear it.

"Think we should go?" asked Fetterman, draining his beer.

Gerber nodded and then saw Robin Morrow. She was a member of the press community in Saigon. A tall, slender woman with blond hair and green eyes, who had attached herself to Gerber a year before. She was wearing a short skirt, a light blouse stained with perspiration and a camera bag. She flopped into a chair, crossed her legs and then leaned forward, her chin on her palm.

Slowly she turned her head, saw Gerber and didn't move for a moment. It was as if she hadn't recognized him. There was a dreamy look on her face, making it seem that this wasn't the first bar she had visited that afternoon.

For a moment Gerber didn't move. He thought about the things they had shared, the adventures and the romance and the anger. He recalled the incident not too long before when she had stripped on the stage of a nightclub in an attempt to get his attention. He remembered how she had gotten drunk with them after the big fight in the Hobo Woods. He remembered washing her back in a shower, seeing the thin network of scars from the whipping she had endured at the hands of a sadistic Vietcong officer. They had shared so much over so many months, and yet remained strangers.

Before he could move or say anything, Morrow was on her feet, staggering toward him. She dropped into a vacant chair at his table. "Captain Mack Gerber, officer extraordinaire."

"Hi, Robin."

"Hi, Robin," she mimicked. "That all you can think of Captain Mack Gerber?"

"Can we get you a drink?" Fetterman piped up, smiled and added, "Although you don't seem to need one."

"Sure, I'll drink," she said, turning her head toward him in an exaggerated movement. "Anything with alcohol in it. Except a damned beer. Not enough kick in the damned beer.'' She leaned her elbow on the table, slipped off and sat up as if nothing had happened.

Fetterman got to his feet and said, ''I'll see what I can do for you.''

Morrow nodded at him, and then ducked her head as she swiveled around so that she could stare at Gerber.

Her eyelids moved up and down with considerable effort, as if she might fall asleep any second. And Gerber was certain that she wasn't very far from it. ''Never called me for that dinner you promised. Let good old Colonel Bates take us to dinner once, but you never called. Went to dinner with Tony, but not you.''

''Hell, Robin,'' said Gerber. ''I've only been back in-country a couple of weeks.''

''Never called,'' she repeated. ''Promised, but never did. Tony called, but you never did. Probably called my sister, though. Probably called Kari.''

Gerber felt his stomach grow cold. He took a deep breath, giving himself a moment to think. Robin and her sister. What a pair they had turned out to be. Gerber had fallen for the sister and when she deserted him, had taken up with Robin. It had seemed a bad idea at the time and it had gotten worse over the last few months.

''I haven't talked to your sister for a couple of months,'' said Gerber. ''She doesn't even know I'm here.''

Robin laughed, nearly doubled over, her arms wrapped around her stomach. ''Ho, that's good. Bet Kari's so pissed she can't see straight. That's very good.''

Fetterman reappeared with a drink in hand and set it in front of Morrow. ''You really think you need that?'' he asked.

''Hell, Tony,'' she said. ''No one needs a drink. I want it, okay with you?''

''Drink up,'' he said.

"Drink up," she repeated. She wavered for a moment, as if about to fall from her chair. When Gerber reached over to hold her up, she said, "Oh, you can touch me. I don't have the plague. That's fucking nice."

"Look, maybe we'd better get out of here," said Gerber.

She smiled lewdly and leaned toward him. She pulled at the top of her blouse, revealing her cleavage. "You got some plans, Captain Mack? Going to take the drunk to your room?" She seized her drink, spilling some of it on the table.

"Captain," said Fetterman, "you'd better get her out of here. There's no telling what she might do." He spoke quietly, as if she wouldn't understand his words.

Gerber got to his feet and took her elbow while visions of her striptease in the club in downtown Saigon danced in front of him along with the confrontation outside on the street. He had tried to cover her with a jungle jacket while she had shouted at him and a group of GIs had stood around watching, a few of them clapping.

"Come on, Robin, let's go."

"Where we going, Captain Mack?" She picked up her cocktail and drank half of it. She slammed it to the table, spilling the remainder.

"For a little walk. Give you a chance to sober up," he said, lifting her to her feet.

She fell into his arms and looked up at him. "Okay, Captain Mack. Anything you want."

Almost supporting her full weight, he guided her out of the bar and into the hotel. They crossed the carpeted floor of the cavernous lobby, past the Vietnamese-French bell captain who grinned his approval, and into the elevator, which was a gilded cage that rose through the interior of the hotel.

Once upstairs, Gerber guided Morrow to his room, unlocked the door and helped her inside. While she leaned against the wall, Gerber closed the door. A moment later he heard a thud and turned to find Morrow sitting on the floor, her legs spread and her skirt hiked, revealing her cream-colored underwear.

"Now what, Captain Mack?" she asked innocently. "What you got on your mind?"

"Oh, God," he moaned, knowing that anything he said would be wrong. He reached a hand out and said, "Let me help you to your feet."

"If you insist."

Gerber hauled her up and maneuvered her toward the bed. As they approached it, she turned around so that she faced him. Looking over her shoulder, she saw the bed and fell back, sitting on it.

"What now, Captain Mack?" she asked. Although her speech in the bar had seemed slurred, now it was precise. She held herself upright, in a stiff, unnatural posture, as if to prove that she wasn't drunk or that it had all been an act to get him to take her to his room.

"I think you need some rest," said Gerber, looking down at her.

"Rest," she said, nodding. She looked at her chest and began to fumble with the buttons of her blouse. "Can't sleep in my clothes. Get them wrinkled."

"Robin, why don't you lie down and catch a nap. You need it."

Instead she stood and stripped her blouse from her shoulders. She held it wrapped around her upper arms, barely covering her breasts as she winked at him, her tongue in the corner of her mouth. Then she dropped the blouse, unfastened her skirt and let it fall so that she was standing in front of him in her panties and bra.

She turned slowly, arms on her hips, showing him her body. She stumbled and caught herself. Then she faced him. "What d' you think, Captain Mack. Better than my stuffy old sister, don't you think? Firmer. Smoother. Softer. She's got a big butt." She began to giggle helplessly, sat on the bed hard, and repeated herself. "Got a big butt. Old Kari has a fanny and a half."

Although Robin was giggling, Gerber could detect a maliciousness under her words. He studied her carefully, the light coating of sweat that made her skin shine, the way sweat-damp bangs brushed her eyes, and the sexuality that she exuded right now.

He moved toward her and pushed on her shoulders, forcing her to lie back on the bed. She grabbed his wrists, her fingernails digging into his skin.

"Robin, I think you should take a nap and then we'll talk."

"Sure we will, Mack. You always say that and then you weasel out of it."

"Not this time." But he knew he would, just as he had a dozen other times. That was the thing about drunks. They often spoke the truth. No longer inhibited by the social norms, they felt free to speak things that they would never say if they were sober. Robin was right when she said that he managed to get out of the situations without talking to her as he had promised. He'd done it so often that it was becoming second nature.

He was about to say something when she rolled to her side, tucked her hands between her thighs and let out a ragged snore that might have been a partial sob. Her body jerked once, as if to shake off the effects of the alcohol, or the war, and then she was still.

"Oh, Robin," he said, amused by her. He jerked the bedspread across her curled form to protect her from the air-conditioning. Satisfied that she'd be okay, he went into the bathroom for a drink of water. He sat in the wing chair, watched her sleep for a few minutes. As the sun disappeared and darkness descended on downtown Saigon, he sipped the water and wondered what would happen when she woke.

3

THE CARASEL HOTEL
SAIGON

Robin was still asleep when Gerber woke. Spending the night sitting in the chair with his feet propped on the end of the bed hadn't been the most pleasant he had passed in Vietnam. But then, it wasn't the worst, either.

Robin had wakened during the night, sick from all the alcohol that she had consumed during the day. She had stumbled toward the bathroom, moaning to herself, and calling Gerber's name. A light sleeper himself, he had awakened instantly to find her sitting on the floor, her head resting on the toilet seat. Her skin had an unhealthy pallor to it. He had managed to sit beside her and hold her while she puked. With a damp towel, he had wiped the perspiration from her face and the vomit from her chin.

When she was ready to go back to bed, he helped her to her feet, had gotten her a glass of water to wash out her mouth and silently guided her into the other room. As she climbed into bed she looked at him and mumbled, "So sorry." Her voice was soft, quiet.

In the dim light filtering through the window, he had studied her face. There was a glint of brightness at her eyes, as if they had filled with tears. Gerber sat on the bed, held one of her hands and told her not to worry about it. Everyone got drunk once in a while.

She pulled her hand free and rolled over, her back to him. As she closed her eyes she said, quietly, "I didn't think you'd understand."

Now it was morning. Gerber looked at his watch. It was nearly seven. He padded into the bathroom and shut the door. Quickly he shaved, brushed his teeth and combed his hair. Back in his room, he put on his jungle fatigues, and picked up his socks and boots. From the wardrobe shoved into a corner, he retrieved his rifle. He left the room and finished dressing in the hall, ignoring the amused stares of a couple of Air Force sergeants and their whores.

Fully dressed now, he took the elevator down to the lobby and then dropped into one of the chairs to lace up his boots. He had almost finished when a shadow fell across him.

"Morning, Captain," said Fetterman. "How is Miss Morrow?"

"How would I know?" asked Gerber.

"The two of you left together fairly early and neither of you reappeared. The conclusion is obvious."

"Okay, Sergeant Obvious," said Gerber, "Miss Morrow is asleep in my room where she passed out soon after we got there last night. She was out all night, except for the hours when she was sick."

"And she's there now?" asked Fetterman.

"Still asleep. She's going to wake with a big head. She was bombed out of her tree."

"Well, it's just as well," said Fetterman. "We're due over to MACV Headquarters in about an hour."

"Shit! What the hell for?"

"I don't know. Talked to Maxwell and he has to see us right now. Wouldn't give me a clue, but said it was important."

"Just great." Gerber sat up, looked at his fingernails.

"We've time to eat breakfast first, if you want," said Fetterman.

"Let's just go see Maxwell. Maybe he'll have some doughnuts for us. If not, we can grab something in the cafeteria over there." Gerber grinned. "Besides, with Westmoreland running around MACV, the food should be good. They won't want to offend the general."

"It's still a mess hall, Captain."

"How could I forget?"

Outside the hotel they found a taxi, an old Chevy that was a riot of color, having been partially repainted half a dozen times. The interior smelled of cigarette smoke and vomit. The seats were stained in a dozen places and the floor littered with crushed cigarettes, candy wrappers and a used condom.

The driver was a burly South Vietnamese who sported a stubble and understood almost no English. He grinned at them, showing a gap where his front teeth should have been and nodded vigorously when Fetterman mentioned the MACV compound. Gerber instinctively knew that the man would have a Kamikaze complex.

They roared off, scattering a couple of pedestrians and barely missing a young woman carrying an armload of packages. They weaved in and out of the traffic, sliding into gaps that were almost too small for the car. Once he had the destination in mind, the driver kept both hands on the wheel, using the horn more often than the turn signal or brake.

They raced up wide boulevards, past palm-lined lawns of government buildings, then down narrow streets jammed on each side with squalid hovels. The cardboard and plywood structures were taped and nailed together haphazardly, unable to withstand the first of the coming monsoons; low, dirty buildings with wires strung between them or dangling from poles that looked ready to fall. The streets were muddy and lined with garbage. The open sewers reeked of refuse.

Then they burst onto a wide street, fell in behind a convoy of U.S. Army trucks, driving in the diesel stench of the engines until their driver got impatient. Leaning on the horn, he roared around them, causing a Vietnamese traffic cop to seek refuge behind the middle-of-the-road traffic light.

Finally they slid to a halt in a cloud of gravel dust in front of the MACV complex. The driver turned, one arm on the back of his seat, grinning as if he had won the Indianapolis 500.

"You pay me now!" he said. "One thousand P."

"No good. Numbah Ten Thou," said Fetterman. "One hundred P at most."

"You GI *dinky dau*. You pay me now. One thousand P. Good drive. You like."

Gerber couldn't help laughing over Fetterman's haggling. The driver wanted less than ten dollars for the trip for the two of them. If he had been a ride at an amusement park, he would have been worth the money.

"I give you two hundred. No more." Fetterman looked grim. Determined.

"Eight hundred," said the driver, his face becoming a tight mask.

"Too much. Too much. I give you three hundred and a tip of fifty P."

"Six hundred," said the driver, looking as if he had lost his best friend.

"Five," said Fetterman.

"Five!" said the driver, shouting. "Five hundred P and tip."

Fetterman took out his wallet and counted out the money. He handed it over to the driver who was happy again.

As he got out of the cab, the driver called, "Hey, GI. You numbah one! Good Joe."

Gerber, who was standing on the sidewalk that led to the building, had a smirk on his face. "Come on, Joe. We don't have all day."

"Be right with you, Captain." He watched the taxi rocket off, nearly crippling a couple of MPs who flipped him the bird. Then the vehicle disappeared in a cloud of dust around a corner.

"The man was phenomenal," said Fetterman. He turned, squinted in the bright morning sun and added, "That was a fine piece of driving."

"Then why argue the price down?" asked Gerber as they started toward the building.

"Because the price was too high for here. I pay it and the next guy then has to pay it and we have runaway inflation. Everyone thinks he should have more money. I argue him down to a more reasonable price, then prices remain low and everyone is happy."

They reached the first set of large glass doors. "Nice of you to worry about the Vietnamese economy that way, Tony," said Gerber, bowing slightly and ushering Fetterman through with a sweep of his arm.

Fetterman grabbed the inner door and did likewise for Gerber. The air-conditioned air hit them like a hard November wind. Gerber shivered as he stepped into the building.

"Just doing my bit, Captain," Fetterman said. "If we'd provide our troops with a little cultural training, perhaps teach them a little about the Vietnamese people before they got over here, we could avoid some of the problems we run into. Wouldn't have our soldiers trampling on Vietnamese beliefs and traditions without realizing they were doing it.''

"I don't need a lecture on Vietnamese culture, Tony," said Gerber.

"Yes, sir."

They walked along the tiled hallway, looking at the posters on the bulletin boards, the photos of the presidents of the United States and of Vietnam. Pictures of the military chain of command, from the Chairman of the Joint Chiefs of Staff, down to the local men. They didn't speak to any of the men or women who were hurrying along the hall, all looking grimly determined while clutching bundles of paper as they rushed from one office to the next. Some wore starched jungle fatigues, others were dressed in civilian clothing and a couple in Class A uniforms.

They reached a stairway that led down to a lower floor. There, they were barred by a floor-to-ceiling iron gate, which was guarded by an MP who wore a shiny black helmet liner and a .45 on his hip. They stopped outside of the gate, Gerber produced his ID card and told the man that he was expected inside. The guard used a field phone to confirm Gerber's clearance into the restricted area, checked Fetterman's ID and watched while both men signed in. Then he opened the gate and directed them to the proper office. He carefully locked the gate behind them.

Gerber and Fetterman turned down a corridor lined with cinderblock walls that were damp with condensation. Rust spots, where metal furniture or file cabinets had been and later moved, stained the green tile floor. Finally they stopped in front of a wooden door that had no markings other than a small, black number at eye level. When Gerber knocked, the door was opened.

Jerry Maxwell stood there, looking as if he had been up all night. He stepped back and waved them into the office.

Inside was a disaster area. One wall was lined with file cabinets, the tops covered with file folders, loose papers and boxes of material. A massive cabinet squatted in a corner, a combination lock on the second drawer. A battleship-gray desk, the top littered with more papers, documents and file folders, was pushed into another corner. One side was lined with a wall of Coke cans nearly two feet high. A small chair sat in front of the desk and a larger one next to it. A single picture with its glass broken hung on the wall. Under it was a stack of framed pictures showing U.S. Cavalry men fighting the Cheyenne Indians in the Hayfield Fight.

The subterranean office had no windows and was therefore lit with fluorescent lights. The air, super-cooled by the massive air-conditioning system on the roof of the building, threatened to freeze everything solid.

Maxwell closed the door and gestured at the chairs. "Please. Sit down." Then he leaped in front of Gerber and plucked his wrinkled suit coat off the chair reserved for visitors.

"Excuse the mess, but I've been up all night trying to get this thing coordinated. We don't have a lot of spare time."

"Jerry," said Gerber patiently. "I've told you this before. First you ask us how things are. We chat for a moment and then you chop us up with your impossible request."

Maxwell leaned a hip against the desk and then shoved some of the paper out of the way so he could sit down. "I'm in no mood for your lectures on manners, Captain."

"Sorry, Jerry," said Gerber, taking the chair vacated for him.

"I told you I've been up all night working on this. We don't have a lot of time to fuck around on it. You've got to have your team ready to go by zero three hundred tomorrow."

"Well, Jerry, I was up most of the night, too, so I'm not impressed with that." Gerber smiled. "Of course, my reason was probably more pleasant than yours."

Maxwell pinched the bridge of his nose. "If you're done, I'd like to get down to business."

Fetterman picked a folder with a bright red secret stamp on it from the desk. He flipped it open and began to read it. Maxwell grabbed it out of his hands and slammed it onto a pile of other secret material.

"You guys through clowning around?"

Gerber shrugged and looked at Fetterman. "You done clowning around Master Sergeant?"

"I don't know. You?"

"Yeah, I think I am. Okay, Jerry, fill us in on the big project that kept you up all night."

"Are you gentlemen familiar with the air war being flown over North Vietnam?"

"Only that we've got bombers and fighters going in there day after day and that our Secretary of Defense is doing all he can to make sure that the bombing does no grave injury to the enemy," Gerber said glibly.

"Now what in the hell does that mean?" Maxwell appeared to be momentarily distracted.

"It means that the Secretary of Defense has ordered that our pilots avoid certain targets like the manufacturing centers in Hanoi, small though they may be, and the harbor at Haiphong. Heaven forbid we might sink a Russian ship offloading war supplies for the communist forces."

Maxwell shook his head. When he spoke again his voice sounded tired. "There are good political reasons for those orders. Reasons that the men in the field might not be fully cognizant of."

"Fine, Jerry," said Fetterman. "I'll tell the men who are being shot at with those weapons and ammunition that there are reasons for it that they aren't fully cognizant of. I'm sure it will make them feel better.''

"Can we get on with this?" Maxwell was beginning to get testy. "Or are you two planning to play Mutt and Jeff for the rest of the morning?"

"Look, Jerry," said Gerber, "it's very hard for us to sit here and listen to this bullshit. That we can't do something because it might violate some stupid guideline some ignorant politician thinks is a good idea. Not when there are people out there shooting real bullets at us."

"Okay, okay," said Maxwell. He stood and shuffled over to the file cabinets. He turned, leaning back on them and said, "I have a mission for you two. You'll have to move quickly, and given what you've said, I think you'll go for it."

"Tell us, Jerry," said Gerber.

"First you have to agree that everything you hear in this room from this point on goes no further than this room. That's the guideline on this."

"You know that we don't talk out of school," said Gerber. "Go ahead."

"Okay," he said, and then launched into a tale about the Wild Weasels, the air war being fought over North Vietnam and the sudden development of a missile system that seemed to use something other than radar for acquisition and guidance. He explained the prevailing feeling that because of this new development the balance had been tipped in the enemy's favor and that U.S. involvement in the air war was at a disadvantage.

"The most worrisome thing," continued Maxwell, "is that all indications are the missiles are being launched from SA-2 Guideline sites."

"Guideline?" said Gerber.

"The NATO name for the SAM missile. SA-2 Guideline. Anyway, prior to a couple of days ago, all these missiles used radar for target acquisition and guidance. We could counter that, but now they seem to be launching missiles that don't use radar and that negate our Wild Weasels."

"The missiles are coming from the SA-2 sites?" A frown appeared on Fetterman's face.

"Yeah. That's the problem. No indications from the launch site that they're even tracking and suddenly our fighters have a missile flying up their tailpipes."

"So the assumption," said Gerber, "is the Soviets have developed a new tracking and guidance system and given it to the North Vietnamese."

"Yeah."

"And to defeat this system," said Fetterman, "you need a guidance system to study."

"Exactly."

Gerber took over again. "And since all these missiles are deployed north of the UMZ, you want someone to go north to get you one."

"UMZ?" Maxwell looked confused.

"That's what the grunts call the Demilitarized Zone. UMZ for Ultramilitarized Zone, because of all the heavy ordnance both sides have stacked up there."

"Oh, of course. And yes, we want someone to go north and get a guidance system. But it's not quite the hit-and-miss proposition that you might think. We have identified the sites where the new missiles are deployed so that we put you down close to one."

"Why not just bomb the shit out of them?" asked Fetterman. "End of problem."

"Not really," said Maxwell. "That takes out the site, but doesn't prevent them from using the missiles on a different site or reequipping the old one. If we divert everything to Triple A suppression, then we have nothing left to hit the primary targets, the railroad yards, the bridges, the roads.''

"For the little good it will do," said Gerber.

"The point is," said Maxwell, "we need to know what the new guidance system is like. Once we have that data, we can design a countermeasure that will allow us to carry on the air war."

"Okay," said Gerber, passing a hand through his hair. "When does this boondoggle begin and who do we take with us?"

"The composition of your team will be left to you, unless you wish for me to pull in some people. Tomorrow morning you'll take off for Ubon Air Force Base in Thailand, board a B-52 for a HALO into North Vietnam—''

"Now wait a fucking minute." Fetterman's voice cut through like a knife. "You want us to bail out of a bomber?"

"Perfect cover," said Maxwell. "The NVA won't expect something like that. They'll spot the planes, sure, but they'll know they're bombers that will have a real mission. You'll be jumping from thirty-five or forty thousand feet so they won't know you're on the ground."

"Jesus H. Christ on a popsicle stick." Gerber was incredulous. "The air temperature at that altitude will be thirty or forty below. We hit any kind of upper air winds, we could be scattered all over fucking North Vietnam."

"Admittedly there are a few details that need to be worked out. However, you'll have to use the bombers. Just makes good sense. Puts you into the North with no one knowing it."

"Any more little surprises?" asked Gerber.

Now Maxwell smiled. It was an evil smile that said things were going to get worse. "Just one," he said. "You'll have to take a Kit Carson scout. One who grew up in the area."

Gerber shook his head. "You don't mean...?"

"Of course. Brouchard Bien Soo Ta Emilie. You've worked with her before," he said.

"She's not from the North," said Gerber.

"Oh, but she is," countered Maxwell. He moved back to his desk and dug through the files piled there. When he found the one he wanted, he waved it like a banner. "Says right here that she was born in the North. Debriefing was completed by the CIA, so this is the good stuff."

"Jerry," said Gerber, "do you have any idea of how many different stories she's told?"

"Doesn't matter what's she said to the others," Maxwell said. "This was an interrogation conducted by our people...."

"Oh, well," said Fetterman sarcastically, "then it's got to be right. No one would lie to the CIA."

Maxwell ignored the comment. "Okay. You have until five this afternoon to get your team together and get over to Tan Son Nhut. I'll meet you over there at Hotel Three and escort you around to the Air America pad. Once there, we'll get you on a flight to Ubon."

"Are there restrictions on the makeup of the team?" asked Gerber.

"None. Whoever you want, within reason. We don't want to take a company in, but we want you to have everyone you're going to need."

"You going to provide us with someone to look at the missile?" asked Fetterman.

"Meaning?"

"Suppose we get up there and onto the site and discover, for whatever reason, we can't get the system out. Shouldn't someone on our team know what to look for?"

"Jesus," said Maxwell. "I never thought of that. Good point. I'll work on that."

Gerber glanced at his watch. "If we're going to pull this off, we'd better get moving. What about transport?"

"I can get you a chopper out of here in ten minutes. It'll be yours all day, take you wherever you want to go. You have any trouble with local commanders, you call me on the lima-lima and I'll have someone call them back within ten minutes with verbal orders. Anything else?"

"Briefings on the local area. Restrictions on our operations. Equipment we're going to take. Extraction plans because I don't want to have to E and E all the way to South Vietnam. Support we can count on..."

"Once your team is set and we know exactly how many are going, we'll get all that taken care of. Finally, intense briefings will be held at Ubon just prior to takeoff. Extraction is being coordinated with the Navy and final plans will be available at Ubon."

"Codes, radio procedures," said Gerber.

"All will be worked out and available at Ubon. Your task, right now, is to put together the team. Everyone you think you'll need and get them back to Hotel Three. I'll approve them at that point."

"Maxwell, if I go to the trouble of getting someone here, I don't want you second-guessing me. If I say I need them, they have to go."

"Okay, Mack," said Maxwell, holding up his hands in mock surrender. "Whatever you want."

"Tony?" Gerber turned to Fetterman.

"I think we better get the show on the road."

"Chopper's on the pad outside," said Maxwell. "I'll get the crew out to it and you can be on your way."

Gerber got to his feet and moved to the door. As he touched the knob, Maxwell said, ''Mack, I'm sorry about that fiasco in the Hobo Woods. That wasn't my fault. I did everything I could for you.''

''Yeah, Jerry, that's what you always say. Well, we'll pull the fat out of the fire again.'' He opened the door and stepped into the corridor.

Fetterman joined him and they walked toward the iron gate. The guard opened it and let them out. Slowly they climbed the stairs, reached the first level and walked to the end of the building. Fetterman opened the door, letting in a blast of hot, humid air. For an instant it was a pleasant sensation after the meat-locker cold of Maxwell's office.

Together they stepped into the bright sun, letting the heat and humidity wash over them like the surf on a beach. Before they had moved more than two steps, they were covered with sweat. Gerber put a hand up to shield his eyes and turned to the single chopper standing on the rubberized pad away from the building. The crew was swarming around it, preparing it for flight. One man was on top, checking the rotorhead, shaking the assembly, looking for mistakes that maintenance might have made.

Gerber stopped short, and watched the activity for a moment. Then he turned to Fetterman. ''I don't like this, Tony. They've thrown it together without thinking it through. Seems to me that having someone familiar with the guidance systems of the missiles on the team should have been the first thing they thought of.''

''Yes, sir,'' said Fetterman. ''That, and finding such a man who is jump qualified. Don't see how they can do it in a couple of hours.''

''That's what I mean. Rush, rush, rush, until we've rushed ourselves out of options.''

''How are we going to handle this?''

Gerber wiped the sweat from his face with the sleeve of his jungle fatigues. "You remember that ranger sergeant in the rubber plantation? You know, the one who was so good. Le Duc or something like that. Why don't you see if you can find him and anyone else who you think might be good?"

"Okay. And what are you going to do?"

"I'm going to get these guys to fly me up to Song Be where Johnny has his camp. See if I can borrow some people from him. I understand he's got Glen Mildebrandt as his exec and managed to get Bocker and Tyme assigned to him. Not sure who all he's got there, but I'm going to borrow the people from him. I think we can trust his judgment."

"How many men do you want me to find?" asked Fetterman.

There was a high-pitched whine and the rotorblades of the chopper began to spin. The noise built into a roar so that Gerber had to lean close to Fetterman to hear.

"You talk to them and then take anyone you think necessary. We can cut it down later, but it'll be better to have too many rather than too few."

"So where'll we meet?"

"Hotel Three, like Maxwell said."

"What about Robin?" asked Fetterman. "She still in your room?"

"Yeah. If I get a chance, I'll give her a call and explain the situation to her. She'll understand."

Fetterman looked at Gerber as if he couldn't believe what the captain had said. "Give her a call, sir. She deserves that at the very least."

"Okay, Tony. I'll see you at Hotel Three."

4

SONG BE SPECIAL
FORCES CAMP B-34

The chopper circled the camp once at altitude, giving Gerber a chance to look at it from the air. Like the old Triple Nickel, it was a star-shaped outpost surrounded by five strands of barbed wire and concertina. The interior was crammed with corrugated tin buildings that caught and reflected the blazing sun. In the center of it was a redoubt with very little empty ground. Buildings and bunkers were jammed into the center.

On the east side of the camp lay a long runway, partially paved with blacktop that turned to a graded slash of red dirt. On the east side of the runway was a helipad and south of that a turn around for airplanes. Outside the wire of the camp was a ramshackle village of dilapidated hootches, open garbage dumps and muddy streets. Most of the montagnards assigned to the camp lived there. In the event of an attack, all the villagers would rush into the camp for protection and to help with the defense.

As the helicopter touched down on the pad, kicking up a swirling cloud of red dirt, a hundred kids ran from the village. Before the rotors had stopped spinning, they had encircled the chopper and were screaming for candy or C-rats or cigarettes. When Gerber refused to give them anything, they melted away as quickly as they had appeared.

He climbed out, but before he could move off, the AC shouted, "You going to be a long time, Captain?"

Gerber turned and stepped up on the skid so that he was looking in the window of the chopper. "Don't know. Why?"

"Well, I just thought that if you're going to be a while, I could get my boys inside and find them a cold drink."

"Fine with me. The aircraft going to be safe here without someone to guard it?"

The AC smiled. "We never leave it alone unless we're on an all-American base. Crew chief or gunner will remain behind. Little later we'll rotate that man so everyone gets a chance to relax inside."

"Just keep your eyes open so that I don't have to go searching all over for you." Gerber dropped back to the ground. A tall, thin officer approached him. He recognized the lopsided gait, the freckled face that was tanned a deep brown. He had an M-16 slung muzzle down over his shoulder. It was hard to see the sun-bleached hair under the green beret molded to his head, but there was no doubt that it was Captain Jonathan Bromhead.

As he neared the chopper, Bromhead called, "Ho, Captain Gerber. Good to see you again." He moved closer, held out a hand and tried to look dignified, but a grin threatened his composure. "Good to see you again, Mack."

Gerber grasped the younger man's elbow, squeezing it. "How's it going out here, Johnny?"

Bromhead said quietly, "They call me Jack here."

"Okay, Jack, how's it going?"

Bromhead waved a hand and said, "We've got a good camp. Patrol the mountains to the east, hunting the VC and NVA. Get mortared once a week or so, but no real problem with that. The locals are good in a fight. Only trouble is when they bring in the Viets. They can't get along with the Yards so we have quite a bit of tension.''

"At least the VNAF stopped dumping their bomb loads on the Yard villages.''

"Yes, sir. You want to stand out here in the hot sun talking Vietnamese politics or you want to come on in and take a look at my camp?''

"Take the tour, of course," said Gerber.

They crossed the runway that miraculously hadn't been ruined by peta-prime and walked up to the gate. Gerber was surprised at how small the camp was. Unlike the Triple Nickel, which had nearly seven hundred soldiers living inside, most of the camp's defenders lived in the village. Since the defense force was smaller, the camp was designed so that fewer men could hold it. From the front gate, Gerber could see into the redoubt. Although there were a couple of large, tin buildings inside, they were almost completely underground with sandbagged steps leading down to them.

"New idea," said Bromhead. "Makes the mortar attacks less effective because the shrapnel goes through the roof without hitting anything.''

"What about the direct hit?''

"No problem. We've a layer of sandbags rigged in the ceiling so they absorb everything. A rocket is a different story, but Charlie doesn't fire that many at us and usually misses the camp altogether.''

"Looks good," said Gerber.

"Come on. We'll go to the team house. Last time I saw Bocker, he was in there drinking beer and complaining about the heat. He'll probably want to say hello to you.''

As they moved toward the redoubt, Gerber asked, "You got Tyme here?''

"Sure. He's out on the perimeter making the monthly check of the claymores."

"I'd like to see him, too."

Bromhead stopped near the door of the team house and searched Gerber's face. "You here on some kind of official business?"

"Uh-huh. I've a mission coming up and I need some help on it."

"So you're going to take my best men and go," said Bromhead.

"That's about the size of it." Gerber stepped down onto the wooden riser that led down into the team house. A wall of sandbags rose on each side to protect the entrance. As he entered he noticed a platform, two feet off the main floor, running around the walls of the team house. There was a series of firing ports near the ceiling so that defenders could shoot at the attacking enemy if they penetrated the wire.

The inside was like any other team house. There were four tables with four chairs around each of them. Red vinyl tablecloths covered each table. A metal pitcher, the outside beaded with moisture, sat on each cloth and place settings in front of each chair. There were bamboo mats on the floors and a few pictures of nude women on the walls, most of them torn from either *Playboy* or *Penthouse*.

The back third of the team house was hidden behind a latticework wall but there was enough visibility to see the stove, sink and refrigerator. Two shadowy shapes moved behind it and there was a clatter of pots and pans.

"Lunch will be served in about thirty minutes," said Bromhead, checking his watch. "You want to join us?"

"Sure. Glad to."

"Why don't you grab a seat and I'll see if there's a cold beer in here somewhere?"

At that moment Bocker appeared through the rear of the team house. He stopped, stared and then yelled, "Captain Gerber!" He rushed forward with his hand out. "Damn, Captain! It's good to see you."

Smiling, Gerber got to his feet and shook hands with the older staff sergeant. Bocker was a burly man, about five ten or eleven and weighed close to two hundred pounds. His light brown hair was close cropped so that the gray invading it would be invisible.

"How you been, Galvin?" asked Gerber.

"Just fine. Captain Bromhead runs a good camp although he's having problems with the Viets, but hell, who isn't?" He saw Bromhead bringing the beers and remembered the old days when Gerber would have beer available at the pre-mission briefings. "What's going on, Captain?"

Gerber accepted a can of beer and jerked the pull tab free. He took a deep drink, rested the can on the table and then slumped into a chair. "Got a deal going on and need some help with it." He shot a glance at Bromhead and then said, "I'm looking for a couple of volunteers. When Justin gets here, I'll let you in on it."

"Then buy me a beer."

"You got it. Captain Bromhead, you heard the man."

"Okay, but I don't want you getting my team drunk."

"I'll keep that in mind."

ROBIN MORROW CAME AWAKE SLOWLY, aware that there was light filtering in through the blinds on the window, aware that her head hurt badly, and not sure of where she was. She tried to remember what had happened the night before, but the only thing that came to her was being hunched over the toilet, throwing up violently. The thought made her stomach flip and her nausea worse.

It was then that she realized she was nearly naked. Involuntarily she pulled the sheet higher up, to her neck as if someone might be able to see her this way. She tried hard to recall what she had done the night before, who she had let talk her into returning to his room.

Cautiously she opened her eyes, saw that she was alone, and threw the sheet off her. She sat up slowly, trying to keep from moaning and wondering why she drank so much. Wobbly, she got to her feet and stumbled to the air conditioner to turn it on. The sudden clatter was almost more than she could bear, but the cold air that blasted out of it made the noise secondary.

She remembered finding Gerber in the bar. Tears stung her eyes. "Damn. Damn. Damn." She sniffed, and rubbed her eyes with the heels of her hands. "Damn you, Mack Gerber."

With a sigh, she stood and padded into the bathroom. She flipped on the light, blinked at the brightness and then leaned forward, studying herself. Her hair was a tangled mess, there were black smudges under her eyes that weren't entirely from the makeup she hadn't removed, and her face looked puffy. With her right hand, she tugged at the skin of her cheek, smoothing it.

"You keep drinking like that," she told herself, "you're going to be old before your time."

There was a rumbling in her stomach and she spun, dropping to her knees in front of the toilet. She heaved once, the muscles cramping and forcing, but there was nothing left in her stomach. She dropped her head to her arm, her stomach heaving and heaving and she wished that she could throw up. When the spasms subsided, she rocked to her haunches with her back against the wall, perspiration beaded on her forehead and upper lip. Tears stung her eyes again and tumbled down her cheeks.

After nearly five minutes she climbed to her feet and turned on the sink water. She found Gerber's toothbrush and loaded it with toothpaste. She scrubbed at her teeth and then her tongue until her mouth felt clean. When she finished, she cleaned the brush, left it on the edge of the sink where she had found it.

Back in the bedroom, she looked for a note from Gerber but couldn't find one. She felt sure he would have left her one and looked again. When she didn't find it, she felt the tears again and fought them back. She snatched her clothes from the chair, scattering them on the floor. Bending to pick them up, she started to cry.

"Damn," she said and then began to dress.

DURING HIS FIRST TOUR of duty in Vietnam, Fetterman had seen many of the French forts that dotted the landscape. They were triangular structures that hugged the ground and gave the defenders the best fields of fire. He had walked by them and flown over them, but he had never been inside one.

Now he stood at the gate, waiting for the Vietnamese corporal to open it and let him enter. The chopper that had brought him sat on the pad twenty yards behind him, the rotor blades slowing as the pilot shut down the engine.

The man was waiting until one of his officers ordered him to let Fetterman enter. An officer approached and shouted something in Vietnamese, and the guard opened the gate. Fetterman stepped through, and studied the interior of the fort.

The walls of the bunkers that made up the three sides of the fort were no more than two feet high. Each was topped with barbed wire, and each connected to another with a trench. A network of trenches split the flat, smooth ground on the inside so that there were clear fields of fire in all directions. The fort had obviously been designed with defense in mind. If one wall fell, the defenders could retreat to the trench or one of the other bunkers and fight from there. Each fort was a complex little island that could be cut and cut again, but without the defenders losing the whole thing. Fetterman wondered how well it worked in practice.

The officer stopped near Fetterman, who threw him a salute that could have passed muster on a parade ground. Fetterman normally didn't bother with saluting in the field, but they weren't technically in the field, and sometimes it helped to grease the skids with a little extra military courtesy.

"Good morning, *dai uy*," said Fetterman.

"How may I help you?" asked the Vietnamese captain. He was a short, skinny man with olive skin and black hair. His face was oval and seemed to contain no trace of beard. His brown eyes held only the slightest slant. His English was good but had a French accent to it, which was no surprise to Fetterman.

Fetterman glanced up at the sun, blazing out of a cloudless sky, and then at the open ground to the walls. He shrugged, wishing the man had invited him into the command post. "I was with your men yesterday, during the mission into the rubber plantation."

"Yes?"

"There was a sergeant on that mission," said Fetterman. "A good man and I have another mission for him. Sergeant Duc."

"Sergeant Duc is busy with his duties here," said the captain.

"Yes, sir, I understand that. But if I might have a word with him."

"Follow me," said the officer. He turned on his heel and strode across the hard-packed red dirt.

Several men were sitting in the hot sun, field stripping their weapons. Fetterman and the officer entered a bunker, moving down into the earth. They came to an orderly room, a sandbag lined structure that was noticeably cooler than outside. There was a couch along one wall, a waist-high refrigerator pushed into one corner and a bookcase with Army manuals in the other. Two green file cabinets, both badly dented, stood next to the bookcase. The floor was made of wooden planks and covered with a thin coating of dust. At the foot of the steps was a bamboo mat that had seen better days. Behind a battered, wooden desk sat an American infantry officer. He was wearing faded fatigues with black insignia sewn to the collar. He was a young man with light skin, a huge mustache that violated half a dozen Army guidelines, and eyes that sparkled with a joke that only he knew.

"Can I help you?" he asked.

"Yes, sir," said Fetterman. He noticed the man wore the patch of the Twenty-fifth Infantry Division. Obviously he was an advisor for this group.

"Yes, sir," repeated Fetterman. "There's this mission, and I need to borrow a couple of your people for a couple of days."

The lieutenant nodded and dropped his pencil to the desktop, rocking back in his chair. It squeaked loudly. He slowly laced his fingers behind his head, his eyes locked on Fetterman's.

"Just like that? I assume you have the proper paperwork."

"Well, not exactly. However, I can provide you with a phone number so that you can receive verbal approval to be followed with the paperwork. Orders will be here for you in the morning, though I have to have the men out of here in the next couple of hours. We have a bit of a time crunch.''

The lieutenant sucked in a lungful of air and exhaled. He put his hands on the desk and shoved himself up, grinning. ''If you have that kind of juice, then I don't want to stand in your way. I could get myself into some real trouble. Besides, you Sneaky Petes get everything you want anyway. So tell me, who you after here?''

''Sergeant Duc.''

''Of course. One of the best. Is this a volunteer mission or is he ordered to go with you?''

''Strictly volunteer.''

The lieutenant stepped around his desk. ''Well, follow me and we'll see if we can't find Sergeant Duc.'' He stopped at the steps leading up and asked, ''You looking for any Americans to round out your team?''

Fetterman shook his head. ''Afraid not, unless you happen to be an electronics expert. We're going to need a good man with that kind of background.''

''I can get my stereo to work if that's what you mean.''

Fetterman had to laugh. ''We've something a little more complex in mind.''

''Figured as much.'' The lieutenant turned and walked up the steps.

As they crossed the center of the fort, the lieutenant pointed out various features like a tour guide in a museum. He outlined the visible defenses and suspected staging areas for the enemy if they decided to attack, but told Fetterman nothing about the hidden weapons, concealed strongpoints, or surprises that had been built into the walls.

They were about to step into another of the sandbagged entrances when there was a shout behind them.

''Sergeant Tony!''

Fetterman turned and saw a small man dressed in tiger-striped fatigues. He had dark hair and oval eyes that were cold and hard. He carried one of the old M-1 carbines with two banana clips taped together.

"Krung!"

The lieutenant looked confused. "Do you two know one another?"

Fetterman did not reply while he waited for Krung, his hand outstretched. When Krung took it, Fetterman asked, "What are you doing here?"

"I train Vietnamese. Teach them to kill VC."

"Why aren't you still at the camp? Where's Lieutenant Bao and the rest?"

"Trung uy Bao killed by VC."

"Sergeant," said the lieutenant.

"Sir, is there a place where Sergeant Krung and I could talk? I know him and would like to take him on the mission, too."

"I'll find Duc for you. Why don't you go back to my office and use it?"

"Thanks, Lieutenant."

While the lieutenant went in search of Duc, Fetterman and Krung walked back to the orderly room. Once inside, Fetterman turned to Krung. "Tell me what happened."

Krung dropped onto the frayed couch jammed against one wall. "Bao on patrol with Vietnamese from camp. We out two, three days. We walk into ambush. VC zap us pretty good. Many die on trail but some of us escape."

Fetterman thought of another ambush that had happened nearly eighteen months earlier. The VC had zapped them pretty good then, too. Krung was one of the few survivors that time, fading into the jungle as the VC overran them, killing everyone in sight.

"We go back two day later. We find everyone. They all dead. VC kill them many times. Shoot them many times. Cut them up." Krung's face darkened as he remembered finding the bodies. "They do things to them. Fill their mouths."

Fetterman knew that Krung was groping for the English words to describe the horror he had seen. From what Fetterman knew of VC terror tactics, he was sure that Krung was trying to tell him that the VC had cut off their penises and shoved them in the mouths of the dead. That was a new wrinkle the VC had added in the last year or so.

"I understand," said Fetterman.

"I decide that I kill fifty VC for Trung uy Bao."

"That in addition to the ones you swore to kill for the members of your family?" Fetterman was referring to the pledge that Krung had made when he discovered the communists had killed his family. Fifty of them for each member of his family. And Krung had had a very large family. He had kept score by nailing the genitals of the dead to a board he kept in his hootch. When Fetterman had DEROSed from his first tour, Krung was within twenty or twenty-five of completing that mission. Apparently he had found another.

They talked for a few minutes, and Fetterman learned of the breakup of the Tai strike companies by the Vietnamese command in Saigon. Krung and a platoon of his fellow tribesmen had been assigned to the Vietnamese rangers. Krung didn't like it, but it provided him with the opportunity to kill VC so he didn't complain.

The lieutenant reappeared with an Oriental in tow. "I have Sergeant Duc."

"Thank you, Lieutenant. I need to talk to them in private." Fetterman hesitated and then added, "The mission is classified."

The lieutenant stared for a moment and then said, "Please call me when you're finished. I have work that I have to complete, too."

"Yes, sir. Thank you."

After the lieutenant left, Fetterman walked about the room, checking it, as if looking for hidden microphones. When he had satisfied himself that they were alone, he lowered his voice. "We've been handed a real hot potato. I'll give you some of the details and then if either of you want out, you get out."

Duc sat quietly, first staring at Krung and then at Fetterman. "Why me?" he asked.

"Because we need at least one Vietnamese on the mission and you demonstrated an initiative yesterday. Are you jump qualified?"

"As ranger it is necessary to learn how to use parachute. I have twelve jumps."

"Good." With that, Fetterman launched into his account of the mission, stopped for a moment and when neither Krung nor Duc asked to be excluded, filled them in with as much detail as they needed. He wanted to let them know what they had let themselves in for by not getting out when they had the chance. He then told them to gather a little of their gear but not to take anything they valued. Weapons, clothing, food and ammo would be provided later. When they were ready, he would meet them at the front gate.

5

AIR AMERICA HANGAR
TAN SON NHUT SAIGON

Gerber, along with Tyme and Bocker who had volunteered
for the mission, entered the corrugated metal hangar. They
crossed the waxed cement floor until they came to a stairwell. The door there held a sign warning that the base
commander could refuse entrance to unauthorized personnel, and that all personnel were subject to search at the
discretion of the base commander.

They climbed the cement stairs, with a metal corner on
the edge of each riser painted yellow. A second locked door
barred their way. This time they knocked and a civilian
peered through a window with a sliding shutter, and let
them in. A second civilian led them down a hallway filled
with steam pipes, electrical wiring and locked access doors.
He stopped and pointed out the briefing room.

Gerber entered first, stopped short and stared at the
people around the table. Fetterman sat there looking cool
and collected. The uniform he wore looked fresh, as if he
had put it on only moments before. Next to him was the
Vietnamese sergeant from the Michelin Rubber Plantation, his fatigue uniform stained under the arms and down
the front. On the other side was a smaller, darker man,

whose black hair was now unkempt. His clothes, the remnants of a U.S. Army fatigue uniform, were frayed, but all the rips had been mended and it was clean.

For a moment Gerber's gaze rested on the smaller Oriental. "Sergeant Krung?"

"I find Sergeant Tony and he invite me to go with you," Krung said.

Gerber moved forward, a hand out. "I'm glad to have you. I think we'll need you on this one." A dozen questions swirled through his mind, from where Krung had been for the last year, to how he was doing with his personal war of vengeance against the Vietcong.

"If you'll take a seat, Captain," said the man at the head of the table, waving at the chairs opposite him, "we'll get this show on the road."

Gerber turned and saw Maxwell sitting at the head of the table. The CIA man was dressed in his usual rumpled white suit with a thin black tie. The knot was loosened so that it hung low. On his right was an attractive Eurasian woman whom Gerber recognized immediately. Her petite form, beautiful face and long black hair attested to her French-Vietnamese heritage. Gerber remembered being entranced by her blue eyes, which appeared to be violet, depending on her mood or her clothing. She wore a flight suit now, with its sleeves hacked off near the elbows. The legs had been rolled up several times so that the cuffs wouldn't drag on the ground.

"Kit?" He had hoped the reluctance he had shown earlier would have convinced Maxwell that she wouldn't be of value on the mission.

"I am going, too," she said, smiling at him. It was something more than just a warm glad-to-see-you smile.

"Maxwell, this is getting a little out of hand." Gerber tried not to stare at her.

"Miss Brouchard was born in the North and will be a valuable asset," said Maxwell, repeating what he had said earlier that day.

Gerber jerked a chair away from the table and dropped into it. He stared at Maxwell. "Miss Brouchard has told so many stories about her background that I'm surprised you accept any of them as fact." He turned toward her. "No offense."

"I understand," she said quietly. "But this time Mr. Maxwell is correct. I was born in the North. You will see that I will be helpful on this mission."

Maxwell glared at him and then gestured at Tyme and Bocker. "If you men will close the door and sit down, we can get this briefing under way. The aircraft, an Air Force C-130, is scheduled for departure in thirty minutes, so we don't have a lot of time—"

"Does the crew have a reason for going, other than to transport us?" interrupted Gerber.

"No."

"Then they're not going anywhere without us, Jerry. Before you start, I want to say a few things about this mission." He looked at Fetterman, then at the others. Tyme and Bocker had slipped into chairs on either side of him, and Kit sat next to Maxwell. Seven people already on the team and not one of them knew what to look for when they got where they were going. Bocker, with his background in electronics and radios, might be trained to understand the guidance system quickly, but that would be at least a ten or twelve-day job, and they didn't have ten or twelve days.

"Isn't someone missing from this group?" asked Gerber.

Maxwell studied each of them again. "No. Everyone's here, unless there's someone you requested and he hasn't arrived yet."

"How about your electronic warfare specialist? I don't see him?"

"He'll meet you in Ubon. Air Force found him and have him there already."

"I assume he's jump qualified. You made sure of that, didn't you?" Gerber turned his attention to Kit. "I assume you are, too?"

"Yes, Captain," she said stiffly. "I have been jump qualified by the Luc Luong Dac Biet. That is the least of your worries."

"And this Air Force puke?" asked Gerber again.

"He is fully mission qualified," said Maxwell. "The Air Force wouldn't have given us someone who isn't mission qualified."

"Meaning you don't know whether he's jump qualified or not," grated Gerber. "Christ, Jerry, I thought after those other fiascos you saddled us with, you'd think this thing all the way through."

Maxwell chose to ignore the remarks. He opened the file folder in front of him. "Final mission briefing will be held at zero two three zero tonight in Ubon. The jump, a HALO mission, is now scheduled to go in at zero four hundred, which should give you over an hour of darkness for cover once you're on the ground."

"Fucking great," said Gerber, sarcastically. Rather than pick up the file folder in front of him, he looked around the conference room. Since it was in the Air America hangar, he had expected something a little nicer than he found, which only proved that the people who fought the war didn't have any of the luxuries of the brass, no matter who they worked for, the CIA included.

The table was scarred with cigarette burns. The ubiquitous water pitcher, this one cracked and empty, sat in the center of it. There were no drinking glasses and the tray that it sat on was dented and stained. Along one wall, which someone had paneled in an attempt to improve the surroundings, was a broken down green couch that was covered with burns, stains and rips. The stuffing hung out in a dozen places. The paneling behind it was warped and nicked.

On the wall opposite Gerber was a recruiting poster that someone had stolen. Under the picture of Uncle Sam pointing out, someone had scrawled in bright red, "I want your fucking ass in Vietnam, now!"

"Actual mission preparation will take place in Ubon," said Maxwell. "I have a few directives that I want to pass along to everyone on the team, and then we'll hustle on down to the airfield."

"I have to make a phone call," said Gerber, suddenly remembering Robin Morrow left behind in his hotel room.

Maxwell looked up startled and then laughed. "You're joking, of course."

"I'm not joking. I have to make a phone call."

"You're making no phone calls, either," said Maxwell. "Now, if you're through with all this other nonsense, I'll finish here and let you go."

When Maxwell finished the briefing, he took them downstairs, through the Operations area of the hangar and out onto the ramp. An Air Force C-130 sat at one end, the doors open and the engines running. One of the crewmen jumped out of the front door near the cockpit, ran around the wing to avoid the propellers, and stopped near Maxwell.

"These the passengers?" he yelled over the roar of the four turboprops.

When Maxwell nodded, the gesture exaggerated, the airman looked at the group and shouted, "Please follow me closely. Watch out for the props."

He led them out of the hot air being blown back at them in near hurricane force by the engines. At the hatch, he helped Kit up the ladder, then waited as each of the men climbed aboard. Gerber glanced up into the cockpit. There was an empty seat across the bulkhead behind the seats for the pilots. When he moved into the cargo area of the plane, he saw the pilots sitting in position, waiting. Neither of them bothered to wave.

Gerber moved to the rear of the plane and stumbled on the rails. These were part of a conveyor system consisting of metal bars with cylindrical rollers between them so that the loaded pallets would slide out of the aircraft easily. Gerber fell, grabbed at the red webbing that was the rear of the seats, steadied himself and moved deeper into the plane. Finally he dropped onto one of the seats and didn't move. The others had already buckled themselves in except for Kit, who climbed over Fetterman and Krung so that she could sit next to Gerber.

The load master circulated, yelling over the noise of the engines that they should buckle in. When he saw they had all complied, he took his seat and buckled himself in.

The roar of the engines increased and the plane began to vibrate. Gerber wiped the sweat from his face. He wanted to talk to Fetterman, to work out the details of the jump and the mission, but the Hercules lurched once and then began moving, sending vibrations through the fuselage. There was a stink of hot oil and burnt jet fuel that made the interior of the plane oppressive.

They stopped moving and the flight engineer came forward with a flashlight, checking the oil levels. A moment later he sat down and the aircraft began its takeoff roll. As the speed increased, the C-130 began to shake and rattle and the hot cargo bay filled with the stench from the engines and heated oil. Gerber tried to keep from leaning with the pressure as the plane rotated and struggled into the air. Kit grabbed Gerber's arm as if wanting protection and squeezed tightly as the C-130 shuddered. There was a whine and a series of bumps as the landing gear came up and almost immediately the flight engineer was moving again, checking various fluid levels.

After a long time it grew cold in the rear of the plane and the heaters kicked in, blowing hot air at them so that their feet froze while they sweated. Gerber unbuckled his seat belt and started to stand. Kit gripped his arm and he leaned close to her so that he could hear what she had to say.

"Where are you going?" she asked.

"Talk to Sergeant Fetterman. I'll be right back. Don't worry," he told her.

He looked at the deck, placed his foot carefully between the rails and the seat and moved to the rear. He sat next to Fetterman and put his lips close to the sergeant's ear.

"Tony," he yelled, "when we get to Ubon, I want you to take charge of this Air Force guy. Find out all you can about him, including whether or not he's jump qualified. I doubt he's HALO-qualified, but who knows?"

"Yes, sir," shouted Fetterman. "Planned on it. You didn't have to come over here to tell me that."

"No, I didn't. Listen, you thought about this HALO out of the B-52?"

"Not much. Just that we'll have to bundle up pretty good so we don't freeze solid and we'll probably have to go out the bomb bay."

"Yeah, that's kind of what I thought. You see any problem with that?"

"No, sir. Just figured we'd drop off the front edge of the bomb bay and free-fall away. I can't see a problem with it, unless they've got a full bomb load and then we'll have trouble, especially if they plan to drop the bombs close to us.''

''We'll have to make sure there are no bombs on this one then.''

''There's one thing I don't like,'' said Fetterman. ''And that's dropping into a DZ where we've had no scouts and we don't have any photos. The terrain could be real shit.''

''Yeah,'' agreed Gerber, his voice loud so that he could be heard over the engine noise. ''Can't be helped. We'll bring that up and see if there's anything they can do for us on that point.''

They sat quietly for a moment, listening to the roar of the engines. Finally Gerber got up and moved back to Kit. She smiled up at him and leaned close so that she could shout over the noise of the engine and the heaters. ''You haven't had much to say to me.''

Gerber nodded in agreement. ''But I haven't had much of a chance.''

''You didn't want me to go on this mission?''

''No, I didn't, but it has nothing to do with you.'' After he had said it, he realized it had everything to do with her. He didn't want to be thrown into a situation where he had to rely on her, although he knew he could. He didn't want to spend several days living in close quarters with her. A woman on a combat mission was a complication he didn't want, especially this woman, although he knew she was capable.

He thought about all that and realized he had shot down all his own arguments. It boiled down to the fact that she was a very attractive female, who had previously shown an interest in him, and that was the complication he wanted to avoid.

She leaned close again, her breath hot on his ear. ''You promised me a dinner and you never delivered it.''

Gerber felt his stomach knot, realizing that Morrow had accused him of the same thing. And both of them were right. He had promised them dinner and hadn't delivered .

She put a hand on his thigh. "It's all right. I understand you have been busy. So have I. But that doesn't mean I didn't miss you."

Gerber leaned against the red webbing of the troop seats and stared at the dull gray of the fuselage's interior. He didn't know what to say. It was almost a repeat of the scene from the night before, except that Kit wasn't drunk and he couldn't escape because he was in an airplane.

He ignored the one comment and responded to the other. "When we get back, I think I should buy you that dinner." He wanted to tell her that they needed to have a talk, but by refusing to talk about it now, he would be adding to her confusion. On a mission like the one they were going on, the last thing he needed was to have any member of the team upset.

Kit laid her head on Gerber's shoulder, looked up at him for a few minutes and then went to sleep. He wasn't sure what he was going to do. He couldn't afford to worry about her emotional state as they prowled the forests of North Vietnam.

He decided he'd have to do something to set the record straight the first chance he got. An airplane heading to Ubon carrying the rest of his team was not the place.

And then he realized that Maxwell had managed to railroad them out of the hangar before he had a chance to call Robin. She was probably madder than hell about that.

ROBIN MORROW STOOD OUTSIDE Gerber's hotel room and knocked. At first, she tapped lightly on the door, almost afraid someone would hear her. Then she knocked harder, slamming her fist into the wood, rattling the door in the frame. When someone across the hall opened his door and stuck his head out, she grinned sheepishly and shrugged at him.

If there was someone in Gerber's room, he wasn't answering the door. She waited a few seconds longer, embarrassed by the stony silence coming from the room. Finally she turned and walked down the hallway, her footsteps muffled by the stained and torn maroon carpet. When she reached the gilded elevator cage, she noticed exactly how shabby the hotel looked. Marked walls, ripped wallpaper and peeling paint. In its heyday it might have been a first class hotel but it had degenerated into a second class apartment building housing soldiers, airmen, and marines, many of whom didn't have the opportunity to stay the night very often.

As she left the elevator she noticed two civilians standing next to the door that led to the bar. Smiling, she approached them, thinking incongruously that their attire, sweat-stained khakis, was becoming the uniform of the American press corps. One of them wore a shirt with loops above the breast pocket. The loops were designed for the large caliber bullets used to kill big game on African safari. But the tunic had become fashionable with journalists in the tropics.

"George. Peter," she said, nodding at them.

George Krupp, the larger and older of the two, pushed at the door, holding it open for her. He had thinning, gray hair and a bald spot on the top of his head, which glowed red from too much time in the sun without a hat. His skin was unusually pale despite the time in the sun, as if he was sick to his stomach, but his brown eyes were clear. A network of red lines crisscrossed his nose, indicating that he spent more time writing his stories in the bar than in the office.

"Care to join us?" he asked, nodding at the bar. "Thought we'd grab a quick one before sallying out to find some food."

"Thank you," she said as she passed him. "Don't mind if I do."

Peter Latham had thick black hair that was fashionably long, hiding the tops of his ears. Robin knew that he thought of himself as some great adventurer, someone who didn't let obstacles stand in the way of the story. Yet his youth, the long hair, thick eyebrows, and almost delicate features suggested something else about him. He was a skinny man whose deep tropical tan stopped at his neck and shoulders so that only his face and arms were brown. Robin knew that he was embarrassed by the lack of muscular development on his body so he refused to wear shorts or go without his shirt.

He held a chair out for her and she took it. "Thank you, Peter."

He slipped into the chair next to her and leaned forward, leering. "The great warrior hasn't returned, huh?"

"Nope. Still missing."

Peter sat back, looked at George, who was signaling for a waitress. "If it was me, I'd be trying to find out where he is."

George had caught the attention of a Vietnamese girl who looked hot and miserable. Her hair, nearly waist long, was sweat damp and there were large stains under her arms and down the back of her skimpy blouse. She slid close to them, smiled weakly because she didn't have the energy to waste on useless flirtation.

George ordered beers for everyone and sent her off with a solid smack on her backside. She didn't react, already used to the crude behavior of the American press and too tired to care.

"Now," said George, turning his attention back to the people with him, "you say this captain left early and hasn't returned. Left you no note or anything."

"I never said all that." Robin felt as if her privacy had been invaded by George. He leaped to conclusions on the barest of information. The unfortunate thing was that he was right too many times.

"Okay," he said, slapping his hands together and rubbing them briskly. "I think your captain left you in the morning, assuming that he would be back before you woke up, or at the very least, before you got out of the room this morning. That's why there was no note."

"I like that," said Robin. She liked it more than she cared to admit to either of the men with her. It was what she herself had thought and it was what she hoped was true.

"Then," continued George, "he planned to call you, but found that was impossible."

"Now why is that?" asked Peter. "Telephones all over Saigon. It's not like we've fallen off the edge of the earth."

George turned to face him. "No. But Robin's captain might have. You're assuming that he's still in Saigon, but there's no reason to assume that. Given the way some of these guys work, I wouldn't be surprised to learn that he's in North Vietnam now." He grinned as if in on some private joke.

"Oh, come on," said Robin.

"Maybe not North Vietnam," said George, "but the point is, he's out of Saigon now, doing who knows what."

Robin was going to protest that, too, but the waitress arrived. She carefully avoided getting too close to George, set beers on the table and tried to retreat, but George was too fast for her. He waved a five dollar bill at her. Not MPC, the military payment certificates that were periodically changed to ruin the black market, but a real American greenback. She moved toward him, endured George's hand on her backside, and then snagged the bill.

As she disappeared into the crowd, Robin said, "Most bases have a field phone connection to Saigon."

George drank half his beer in a hasty, noisy gulp, leaving foam on his upper lip. "Who said he was on a base. Hell, Robin use your head. The poor man could be ass deep in mud, miles from a phone. This isn't like he's an errant husband who hasn't taken the trouble to phone. Besides, that field phone connection doesn't give him a phone from which to call you. It just gives the base commander the opportunity to talk with someone at MACV Headquarters if he has to."

She took a sip of her beer before speaking again. "Why are you going to such lengths to protect him?"

Now George grinned. "All part of the plot, my dear. First I prove what an understanding guy I am. Next, having disarmed you with that, I propose a dinner. You, thinking I'm harmless, agree. We go to dinner and then—"

"Nothing," interjected Robin, laughing. "Nice try."

"Okay. I fall back to my second position and ask, what in the hell is so important that he doesn't even have a chance to call the girl he left? The girl who, the last time he saw her, was puking up her guts—"

"Now how in the hell did you know that?"

"Elementary, my dear Robin. I saw you yesterday, pretty well blitzed. I saw you stumble into work this morning, wearing the same clothes you had on last night, looking as if the world was going to end and pissed that it hadn't happened yet. Now you turn up here, dressed in your fineries, looking radiant, obviously to rub out yesterday's image."

Robin glanced down at her silk blouse. She picked at the shoulders with her thumbs and index fingers, pulling it away from her sweat damp body. "This old rag?"

"Is marvelous," said George.

"Glad someone likes it."

"I think it's beautiful," said Peter, feeling left out of the conversation.

"But more importantly," said George, "is where the hell did your captain get to and what the hell is he doing?"

"I don't know," said Robin.

"Well, my dear, if you'll agree to that dinner, we'll work on that problem for two reasons. One is that you want to find him again, and two, I think he's at the heart of one hell of a good story."

IT WAS DARK when the C-130 touched down on the runway, bouncing high and dropping back in what was probably the worst landing ever made at Ubon. It wasn't totally the pilot's fault. He had to land in the middle of a thunderstorm that hovered over the field with winds in excess of forty miles an hour. The lightning kept blinding him, the radar and ILS had failed and if he hadn't been ordered to get the damned plane on the ground, he would have circled far to the south, waiting for the storm to spend itself.

They taxied through the howling wind and the driving rain, the interior of the plane lighted only by the storm. The aircraft rolled to a stop and the load master opened one of the rear doors, pushing it up and out of the way. The moment he did, the swirling rain whipped in with the hot, humid air of Northern Thailand.

Outside, on the taxiway was a solitary man holding a flashlight. He wore a regulation military rubberized poncho that was trailing behind him like a thick, useless tail. Behind him was a staff car and a three-quarter-ton truck, each with the engine running and the windshield wipers going at full speed. Their headlights blazed into the night, illuminating the slanting rain as it whipped along the tarmac.

Gerber moved closer to the hatch and looked out. There was no way to get to the car or truck without getting soaked. The engine noise died as the pilot shut down the engines so that the pelting rain drummed on the fuselage.

The man with the flashlight walked to the hatch, stuck his head in and yelled, "Let's hurry it up. Everyone's waiting for you."

Gerber shot the man a glance. "Thanks for the invitation." He turned to the load master. "What are your plans now?"

"We RON here and go back to Saigon tomorrow. I'll be in here along with the pilots for only another twenty or thirty minutes."

"Guess we can't leave the equipment then," said Fetterman, anticipating Gerber.

"Okay," said Gerber, "everyone grab everything and let's hustle to the truck. Tony, why don't you hop into the car with me?"

"Yes, sir."

Gerber moved to the hatch, staying to one side, out of most of the rain. He put a hand up to shield his face, saw the dome light in the car come on and leaped through the hatch. He hit the tarmac, slipped and twisted his body to correct his balance. His boots splashed water in the puddles as he jogged through the pelting night rain and skidded to a stop near the rear door of the car. It popped open and he ducked inside and slammed the door.

"Christ, that's a monsoon."

"Close to it, Captain."

Terrorists, anarchists, hijackers and drug dealers—BEWARE!

In a world shock-tilted by terror, Mack Bolan and his courageous combat teams, *SOBs* and our new high-powered entry, *Vietnam: Ground Zero* provide America's best hope for salvation.

Fueled by white-hot rage and sheer brute force, they blaze a war of vengeance against a tangled international network of trafficking and treachery. Join them as they battle the enemies of democracy in timely, hard-hitting stories ripped from today's headlines.

Get 4 explosive novels delivered right to your home—FREE

Return the attached Card, and we'll send you 4 gut-chilling, high-voltage Gold Eagle novels—FREE!

If you like them, we'll send you 6 brand-new books every other month to preview. Always before they're available in stores. Always at a hefty saving off the retail price. Always with the right to cancel and owe nothing.

As a subscriber, you'll also get…
- our free newsletter *AUTOMAG* with each shipment
- special books to preview and buy at a deep discount

Get a digital quartz calendar watch—FREE

As soon as we receive your Card, we'll send you a digital quartz calendar watch as an outright gift. It comes complete with long-life battery and one-year warranty (excluding battery). *And like the 4 free books, it's yours to keep even if you never buy another Gold Eagle book.*

RUSH YOUR ORDER TO US TODAY.

PRINTED IN U.S.A.

Before Gerber could look up, the door was ripped open again and Fetterman dropped in. Rainwater was streaming down his face. He swiped at it, then wiped his hand on his soaked trousers.

"Give it up, Tony. You're soaked through."

Fetterman looked at Gerber, grinning. "Completely, sir."

"Gentlemen," said one of the men in the front, "I understand that you have a number of Vietnamese in your party."

Gerber nodded and stared at the man. "Who might you be?"

"Ah." The man twisted in the seat so that he could hold his right hand out. "Robert Cornett. I work with Jerry Maxwell."

"Well, Mr. Cornett," said Gerber, "we have two Vietnamese and a Nung tribesman. One of the Vietnamese is a Kit Carson scout that Maxwell plants on me every chance he gets. The other just graduated from the ranger's school. Or would in the next few days."

"Yes, well, that presents us with a problem."

Gerber looked at Cornett and then out the windshield. Gusts were rocking the car and the hammering of the rain was making the talk difficult. There was a rhythmic thump of the windshield wipers as they fought the rain. Gerber raised his voice, "Isn't there somewhere else we can talk."

"I have a briefing ready," said Cornett, "but I'm not sure that the Vietnamese should see it."

"Why not?" asked Fetterman. "If you trust them for the mission, there should be nothing in the briefing that they can't see."

"That's the problem…?"

"Fetterman. Master Sergeant Anthony B. Fetterman."

"That's the problem, Sergeant Fetterman," said Cornett. "While you are right about the content of the briefing, it's the source material that I'm worried about."

"Source?"

"Yes, Captain. The information I'm going to give you will have to be disseminated to your men. I don't mind that. Hell, the very nature of the information is so perishable that in a week it won't matter if they're looking at it in Moscow or Hanoi. In a week I'll send it to them myself."

"I wish you wouldn't use the word 'perishable,'" said Fetterman half seriously.

"Ah, yes. Well, hell, in Hanoi they know we're concerned about this new missile. They'd be stupid if they couldn't figure that out."

"So what's the problem?" asked Gerber.

"I have a file of aerial photographs to show you. They were taken by the SR-71, our new spy plane. Taken from nearly a hundred thousand feet and it's like nothing you've ever seen. Like standing on the second floor of a building looking at the stuff. Incredible pictures. I don't want that known in Moscow. That we have that capability."

"My people are trustworthy." There was a finality in Gerber's tone.

"I'm sure they are, Captain, and I have no problem with you telling them everything you know. I just don't want them to see either the photos, or the after-action reports from the pilots on the latest missions."

"I find this all fascinating," said Gerber. "But can we get out of the car and into the building?"

Cornett snapped his fingers and the driver slipped the car into gear. They splashed through the night in silence while wind howled and the rain slammed into them and the windshield wipers shuddered. A few moments later they stopped in front of the Operations building, a sea of light.

The leaves of the palm at the entrance were standing at a forty-five degree angle, attesting to the strength of the wind.

"Before we go in," said Cornett, "I want it understood that the Vietnamese are not to see the photographs or the after-action reports."

"I can understand why you don't want them to see the photographs, but how would the after-action reports hurt?" asked Fetterman.

"During World War Two," said Cornett, "the Japanese launched a series of balloon bombs at North America. These bombs traveled on the jet stream, which they had discovered, and were set so that the bombs would release automatically over the United States and Canada. It was a very successful plan. They started a number of forest fires in the northwest, did some property damage and killed six people in Oregon. The point of this is that the Japanese thought the bombs were falling into the sea harmlessly because there was absolutely no intelligence suggesting they were hitting the land."

Cornett stopped talking for a moment, glanced into the back seat and then continued. "Their plans called for biological warfare to be used once they had determined the effectiveness of the weapons. They would load disease-carrying bombs on their balloons and drop those, except they didn't believe the bombs were hitting the ground. They abandoned those plans. If the enemy finds out how dangerous this new missile is, they're going to deploy it all over North Vietnam. If, on the other hand, they think we're not concerned, they might just avoid the expense of it. What they don't know can't hurt us, just as the balloon bombs didn't hurt us because the Japanese had no idea how effective their bombs were. Hell, the remains of some of them were found as far east as Michigan. It was a very good plan, ruined because their intelligence system broke down.''

"The logic sounds weak to me," said Gerber.

"Granted," replied Cornett, "but the whole point is that we don't have to hand the knowledge to them on a silver platter, either."

"Okay," said Gerber. "I want one of my people in on the briefing and then he and I'll brief the others. I'm not going in without the team fully briefed. You'll have to find a comfortable place for them to wait."

"That's no problem," said Cornett. "We'll stick them in the VIP lounge near Operations here in the hangar until you're ready for them, or they can wait in the break room behind there. They'll be comfortable."

"If I might suggest," said Fetterman, "I'd like to take a look at the parachutes and other gear we'll be using. I don't want to leave all that to someone who isn't going on the mission. Our weapons man will probably want to see the weapons and have them zeroed."

"No time to zero them." Cornett slowly shook his head. "These are good weapons."

"Sergeant Tyme is going to be royally pissed."

"You can tell him the Air Force had one of their weapons people check each of the rifles. They were selected with great care."

"Yes, sir," said Fetterman. "Sergeant Tyme is going to be royally pissed."

Cornett had to grin at that. "Yes, I think I understand. I wouldn't want to go into the field with a weapon that someone else checked for me, especially some Air Force puke. Unfortunately there isn't time to zero the weapons. Takeoff for your mission is in a little more than three hours.

In that time you've got to get briefed, the equipment checked and changed into the new uniforms.''

"Not to mention brief our people, check out the DZ, get the recognition codes for both the ground and air elements, maps and everything else," added Gerber.

"I know all that," said Fetterman, "and I say again. Sergeant Tyme is going to be royally pissed."

6

SAIGON, SOUTH VIETNAM

Robin Morrow was hot and sweaty and had drunk more than she planned to. The night before, when she had been sick in Gerber's hotel room, she had promised herself that she would never drink again. Now here she sat, in the darkness of the outdoor bar, sucking down the beer as fast as either Peter or George would order it for her.

She wiped a hand over her face and then rubbed it against the thin material of her skirt, leaving a wet, ragged stain on her thigh. Her face had begun to tingle, telling her that she was getting intoxicated and even though she had refused the last beer, George had insisted and the waitress had brought it, sitting it in front of her with a smile.

"Dinner," she said.

Peter, who was weaving from side to side while he tried to remain sitting on his chair, and whose eyes refused to focus on the lights of downtown Saigon, giggled and said, "Dinner."

"Yes," said George. "We'll go to dinner in a few minutes. First we must plan tomorrow's attack on the secrecy of MACV Headquarters."

Robin crossed her legs slowly, tugged at the hem of her skirt because it had ridden all the way to mid-thigh. "Why MACV?"

"Use your head, Robin. That's where all the planning takes place, it's where all the secrets are hidden, and it's where we'll find the people we need to talk to."

"You know," she said, leaning forward and setting her chin in the palm of her hand, "Perhaps we should talk to Jerry Maxwell. He's the CIA wheel around here and has been involved in a couple of these messes."

"Shh," cautioned George. "We don't know who might be listening."

"Oh, hell, George, everybody and his brother knows that Maxwell is CIA. The real secret is the name of the Station Chief at the embassy."

"Dinner," said Peter again.

"Okay," said George. "Then we'll go find Maxwell and tell him that we know he's got Gerber on a super-spook mission."

"And tell him that we know Fetterman's been sent on it with him."

"You sure about this?"

"George, if Gerber's on any kind of important mission, then Fetterman is with him. Those two have been together ever since I've known them. They go on R and R together, were assigned to the same base in the States, and were assigned to the same unit over here on their return. Knowing that, we can dazzle Maxwell with what we already know and see what he drops on us."

George clapped his hands and smiled. "My dear, I think you're beginning to see the light. Fuck with their minds and they'll tell you things to try to shut you up. Tell you more because they think they can snow you with just a little bit of the truth, and before they know it, you have the whole story."

"Dinner," said Peter. He picked up his beer, took a swig and tried to set it down. He only succeeded in spilling it. He dabbed at it with the corner of a napkin and giggled helplessly.

"Robin, I really think we ought to pour the poor boy into a cab. You like my play on words there?"

She stood, trying to focus on the bar, which was spinning crazily, the lights blurring and blending until there were only bands of color in front of her. The noise of conversation disappeared, replaced by the driving beat of rock music from a club somewhere down the street. With one hand, she reached out to steady herself, felt her stomach flip over, and promised herself that she *would* never drink again.

"You okay?"

She shook her head gently to clear it, then rubbed her eyes. There was an explosion of colors that slowly faded when she stopped rubbing. When everything focused, she nodded slowly. "Everything is fine."

George helped Peter to his feet and he and Robin supported Peter between them. They walked him into the hotel lobby and out onto the street where they dumped him in a cab, giving the driver instructions on where to take him. George shoved money at him to make sure that Peter got to the right address.

"Now," said George, "that Plan A has succeeded, that is, getting rid of Peter without raising your suspicions, where would you like to eat?"

"I'm not hungry now," said Robin.

George placed a protective arm around her shoulder. "Of course you aren't, but if we don't eat something, the alcohol is going to be absorbed into your system and you'll get sick again. Food will take the edge off, and you'll be ready to see Maxwell early."

Robin only wanted to sit down and rest, but not close her eyes because that made her dizzy and sick to her stomach. If she kept them open, she wouldn't feel nauseous. "If there is something going on, Maxwell will be working tonight."

"Of course, and he'll be there in the morning, tired from a night of no sleep and ready to make mistakes for us to exploit. What we need to do is have dinner and then catch some sleep." He held up a hand and added, "Notice that I said sleep and not go to bed. Wanted you to know that I am as interested in this story as you are."

"I'm not sure how to take that," she said, "but I think it was nice. Okay, let's eat, then hit the sack."

"Right. And trap Maxwell in the morning."

She linked an arm through his, bumped a hip into him and said, "Okay, George. The show is yours. Let's get it on the road."

AT TWENTY-SEVEN THOUSAND FEET, the flight of F-4 Phantoms crossed the coastline of North Vietnam. Slowly, without a command from the lead aircraft, the flight began to separate, each pilot trying to keep an eye on both the jet nearest to him and the instruments in the cockpit. Radio chatter, so much a part of the air war in South Vietnam was unknown in the North. Everyone knew that the North Vietnamese monitored the radio frequencies and sometimes used the transmissions to spot the planes.

Each of the pilots, and the electronic warfare officers in the back seat, knew that the mission was a diversion. They were hanging their butts out for someone else. The Intelligence Officer, giving his portion of the serial lead briefing had known only that they were a cover for another mission. He didn't have any details, but told them that the cover was important. Saigon and Washington wouldn't have risked the flight for some bit of nonsense.

"Of course not," McMaster had said, interrupting. "Those boys in Washington would only risk our lives for important nonsense."

That had brought a laugh from the others, but the Intelligence Officer had only smiled. He shrugged. "I didn't make up the mission profile." He then detailed the known SAM locations, flack batteries, recognition codes for E and E, and gave the SAFE areas. When he finished, he asked for questions, but the men had flown so many missions over North Vietnam that they knew as much about the North Vietnamese capabilities and the locations of those capabilities as he did.

Now the flight leader, Captain Roger Newman, stared through the Plexiglas canopy, watching the flickering lights on the horizon, waiting for them to explode into antiaircraft fire. With a gloved hand, he touched the folded map that was attached to the holder strapped to his thigh and checked his waypoint. They were on time and on course.

A sudden, insistent buzz in his headset made him glance at the instrument panel. The intercom crackled. "Got a high SAM light."

Newman looked out of the aircraft, right and left, and then low, trying to spot the rosebud pattern of the SA-2 site, but even with the bright moon, all he could see was water in the rice paddies and dark stretches of jungle and forest.

"Pods on," he said, telling the aircraft commander of the jet carrying the jamming gear to switch it on. As he spoke, a line of tracers, emerald green softballs, floated upward about a mile away. Nothing to worry about because of the distance.

Almost as soon as he had completed the transmission, the ground in front of him began to twinkle as if someone had set off the longest train of firecrackers in the world. There were flashes of orange in front of him as the rounds detonated. The bursts seemed to be below them, far enough away to be of no threat, indicating the smaller weapons. It would take an 85 mm antiaircraft gun to reach them.

The flight fanned out even more. They began to pick up more SAM lights as the North Vietnamese operators turned on the radar sets. Newman heard the buzz again, but only momentarily as the set was switched on and then off.

More tracers lanced upward, making it look like a second-rate Fourth of July celebration. Cheap fireworks that either burned out quickly, or exploded into yellow-white flashes without the glowing red and green fountains.

"Missile launch," one of the pilots shouted.

Newman looked to the left and then right but the sky was dark. There was nothing on his instrument panel to indicate the enemy gunners were firing at them. To his left the wingman broke down and away, trying to get the missile to follow. At the last moment he would rotate into a rapid climb and hope the missile would slam into the ground before it could turn.

"We have Triple A all over the fucking place," came another radio call. The voice of the pilot was icy calm.

"Roger that. Flight, let's take it up. Begin slow climb...now!"

"Lead, this is Three. I'm hit."

"Roger, Three." Newman turned to look. The single Phantom had shot ahead of him and was climbing rapidly. In the dark, Newman could only see the twin flames of the exhaust, burning a bright blue. The crippled jet seemed to surge forward, bounced once and blossomed into flame. Fire burned on the underside and along the wings. The canopy, now glowing in reflected fire light, exploded away from the plane and then both the pilot and the EWO ejected.

"We have a SAM light," another of the pilots called on the radio.

At that moment the flight began to break up as each of them tried to evade the threats. Newman saw the steady burn of the upcoming missile and turned, diving down at it. He passed it in the power dive, waited and then hauled back on his stick, the G-force crushing him into his seat. A curtain of black rolled down over his eyes, cleared and then returned. He shallowed his climb and then rolled to the right.

Below him there was a plume of yellow-orange fire as the missile crashed into the ground and exploded into a fountain of flame. Suddenly Newman wanted to shout because he had beat that one. Adrenaline surged through him and he felt indestructible. As he stared into the star-studded night sky, he spotted the blazing trail of another missile. In horror, he watched as it closed on the F-4 to his right, which turned and juked, trying to shake the missile's guidance system.

There was another bright flash as the SAM detonated, momentarily blinding him, but as his vision cleared, he saw the Phantom wobbling through the air like a wounded duck trying to remain in the sky. A moment later the canopy snapped back as the crew bailed out and the plane began a slow spiraling dive to the ground.

Newman decided that he had seen enough. On the right was the last of his flight. Together they began a slow turn to the north and kept going until they rolled out on an easterly heading, racing for the safety of the coast and the Gulf of Tonkin.

Over the radio, he called air-sea rescue, giving them the coordinates where his two planes had gone down. He was afraid that they were too far inland to try for a rescue, and he could not stay on station to assist. He reported that all four men had gotten out and that he had seen the chutes, but didn't know if they had reached the ground. There had been nothing on the emergency frequencies yet, but the men could still be trying to get organized.

As they approached the coast they heard the two-tone wailing of a survival radio, indicating that someone, somewhere, had survived the long descent. Newman wanted to turn around and head back, but knew it would do no good. He couldn't help them by running out of fuel over North Vietnam and having to bail out himself. Instead he reported hearing the homing tone of the radio.

When it faded, the backseater touched the intercom button. "I hope that jerk-off Intel guy was right. I hope this was something important."

"Yeah," agreed Newman. "I'd hate to think those guys get a stay in the Hanoi Hilton because somebody in Washington thought it important that we make a nonhostile statement. See, Ho, we can fly over your country any time we feel like it and you can't do a damned thing about it."

He hoped that wasn't the case, but somehow he doubted it.

AT UBON, CORNETT SAT in a small office with both Gerber and Sergeant Tyme, studying the intelligence photos from the SR-71. As they examined the pictures, Cornett was filling them in on the whole plan.

"We got several flights of fighters, both Air Force and Navy, flying over North Vietnam tonight as a diversion. Want the sky filled with activity."

Gerber was sorting through the photos that Cornett had scattered over the table. There were a couple of deep gouges in the wood that had been filled with paint. Gerber sat in one of the wooden chairs that creaked each time he moved. Tyme sat across from him, and Cornett was at the end of the table, flipping through file folders.

The room itself was tiny, the walls and ceiling covered with soft cardboard tile in an attempt to soundproof it. From the outside came the rumble of thunder and an occasional rattle of rain pelting the sheet metal of the roof.

Gerber pulled the map toward him. "Where are the SAM sites in relation to the DZs?"

Cornett took the map, spun it around and then worked his way through the grainy black and white photos. "Okay, most of the DZs are within five to seven klicks of one of the SAM sites we want investigated." He placed a picture on the map and said, "This DZ is actually about eight klicks from the SAM complex here, at Ke Sat. This is one of the places where we had missile launches but no detection."

"Uh-huh," said Gerber. "That's putting us down close to Hanoi and a good fifty miles from the sea."

"Can't be helped," said Cornett. "The other sites are farther inland. There are three of them, any of which is suitable for our purpose."

Gerber took the photo again and bent over it, studying it carefully. The DZ was a wide open field that might have been rice paddies or tilled ground with only a single structure, little more than a farmer's hootch visible. All four sides of the field were bordered by trees, but from the center of the DZ to the nearest tree line was a good klick.

Ke Sat was on a road that linked Hanoi and Haiphong. There was a major river far to the south and another to the north, but neither presented a problem. A couple of small, slender tributaries cut through the trees north and south of the DZ, but they looked small enough that Gerber and his men would be able to cross them quickly.

"What's the traffic like on this road? Looks like a major highway," said Gerber.

"During the day there is truck and foot traffic, most of it light. Some days, after the off-loading of the ships at Haiphong, it can get heavy, but the Vietnamese prefer to use more circuitous routes and travel at night. The road is far enough to the north that it shouldn't interfere with any of your plans at Ke Sat."

"Yeah," grumbled Gerber. "I'll bet."

Cornett started gathering the pictures and stuffed them in a folder. "I take it that you'll be going into Ke Sat."

"I don't know," said Gerber. "Justin?"

"I can't see where it makes a difference, sir. The enemy isn't going to expect us anywhere so we might as well take the site that's closest to the sea and extraction."

"How close to the coast do we have to get for the choppers to come in to get us?"

"Well," said Cornett, a smile on his face, "the Air Force asked that you get to the beach, but I think they'll try an extraction eighty or ninety miles in, if the situation warrants it."

"Why not have the choppers pick us up on the SAM site once we have the information?" asked Tyme.

"Because if you can get to the coast, there is a better than ninety percent chance they can get you out without drawing any fire. The farther inland they have to travel, the more likely it is they're going to get shot at. If no one's chasing you, what's a couple of days in the jungle?"

"You ever been in the jungle, Mr. Cornett?" asked Gerber.

"No, I haven't."

"Well, the jungle is loaded with all sorts of nasty creatures. Carnivorous cats, poisonous snakes and venomous insects. Mosquitoes that could carry off a child. Leeches—

Sergeant Tyme's favorite form of parasitic life. Mammals to bite you and give you rabies. Plant life that can poison you, give you fevers, paralyze you or just make your life miserable. Not to mention that the longer we're on the ground, the better the chance that the bad guys will find us.''

Cornett rubbed a hand over his face in embarrassment. ''I guess I asked for that. At home I spend weeks in the field camping and hiking and hunting. Doesn't seem to be that big a problem.''

''At home, it's not,'' said Gerber. ''But we're talking about the jungle. An environment where a scientist who wanted to discover a new species of animal or plant life could probably waste a week looking for it. What I'm saying is that so very little is known about it that it doesn't resemble your hikes in the friendly mountains or parks in the World. Especially when you throw in a hostile population and enemy army.''

''Well, then, let me rephrase that,'' said Cornett. ''Is it a big problem to try to get off the site before the choppers come in?''

Now Gerber grinned. ''Not really. In fact, it would probably be best for us to get fifteen or twenty klicks off the site before pickup.''

''Good, we can compromise,'' said Cornett. ''If you get clear without pursuit, we'll haul you in before you get to the coast. If the bad guys, as you call them, are chasing you, we'll let the situation dictate the response. If you can shake them on your own, then we'll hold up the rescue. If you're about to be overrun, we'll try to get you out.''

''That's acceptable.''

''Then let's move on. Target is the missile complex at Ke Sat. Now, I have on this piece of paper the radio codes, code words and authentication tables for this mission. Memorize them and then destroy the paper.''

''I'd like my communications man to see that,'' said Gerber.

''Okay, but I want that information destroyed before you hit the DZ.''

For the next twenty minutes Cornett covered the radio frequencies to be used, check-in times, and when instructions or intelligence updates would be broadcast. He explained the coordination for the mission and that while they were on the ground no air strikes or Wild Weasel missions would be directed against any of the antiaircraft defenses around Ke Sat. They would have one week to complete the mission and call for extraction. If they hadn't checked in or been extracted by then, it would be assumed that they were killed or captured and a new mission would be mounted.

''One thing,'' said Cornett. ''I think it is of paramount importance that none of the Americans are captured. The last thing we want is for the North Vietnamese to be able to parade you in front of the world press.''

Before Gerber could respond there was a tap at the door. A moment later an airman dressed in damp fatigues entered and handed a sealed envelope to Cornett. ''Excuse me a second,'' he said as he opened it. After he read the contents, he said, ''That will be all, Airman.''

When the door closed, Cornett said, ''You better make good on this mission. The Air Force and the Navy report heavy losses on the diversion missions. Five planes down, and three others missing.''

''The crews?'' asked Gerber. ''Where are the crews?''

''Reports indicate that some of them bailed out. Chutes were seen.''

"Just what we need," said Gerber. "All the fucking North Vietnamese in the world out looking for downed aircrew, and we jump right in the middle of it. Nice job on the diversion."

FETTERMAN, DRIPPING RAINWATER, was directed through the Operations area and into a back break room. There were vending machines along the rear wall, the fronts brightly lit, offering everything from cold drinks to hot sandwiches. A toaster oven was on a waist-high counter next to the machines. It was flanked by an overflowing waste can. There were a couple of white picnic tables in the room, pictures on the wall torn from men's magazines and aviation magazines, and a musty odor of heavy rain.

There was one man in the room, sitting on a bench in front of a picnic table, drinking Coke from a can. He wore fatigues, the sleeves cut off short and ragged, and the stripes of a staff sergeant sewn to them. He looked up when the door opened, but didn't stand.

The driver of the car pointed and said, "That's Sergeant Barlett. He's the electronics expert for your team."

Fetterman stepped to the table and looked down at the man. He had broad shoulders but there was a roll of fat around his midriff that bulged over his belt. His arms were thick and covered with wiry black hair, but there was nothing about the arms to indicate great strength. The man's face was white, as if he didn't get out in the sun at all. He needed a shave and a haircut and a bath. He had brown eyes that were bloodshot.

"Barlett?" said Fetterman.

"Yeah, I'm Barlett. Who are you?"

"Master Sergeant Anthony B. Fetterman, the NCOIC for this mission."

Barlett took a drink of his Coke and set the can down carefully. "I'm impressed."

Fetterman looked at the driver and said, "That'll be all. Sergeant Barlett and I have some things to discuss."

"Fine. Captain Gerber will be down in a few minutes. Mister Cornett is briefing him."

As the driver left, Fetterman sat opposite Barlett. When the Air Force sergeant tried to pick up the Coke again, Fetterman's hand snaked out, locking itself around the other man's wrist and holding it against the table.

"Oh, now don't tell me," said Barlett. "You're going to prove how tough you are. Well, go ahead and give it your best shot."

"You have jump training?" asked Fetterman.

"What?"

"Jump training? Have you any jump training?"

"Not formal," said Barlett caught off guard. "Civilian training. Skydiving, when I was in college, but nothing in the military."

"That's something, anyway," said Fetterman. "You know what's going on here?"

"I know that you're going on some fucked-up mission to steal a fucking missile or some dumb thing and everyone would like me to go."

Fetterman's grip didn't loosen. He stared into Barlett's eyes and said, "You're going with us and you're going to pull your weight or you're going to die—"

"I don't think so," said Barlett. "You can make me go, but I'm not going to do anything I don't want to. You need me so you'll just have to look out for me. Everyone will have to look out for me."

Fetterman let go of the man's hand and sat back. He grinned and said, "You got that wrong. Hell, the captain and I could steal the guidance system and get it back here all by ourselves. We don't need you. You need us. Now, once we're on the ground, you had better do as we say or I'm going to put a bullet in your head.''

Barlett tried to laugh, but only managed a high squeaky sound. ''You wouldn't do that. You couldn't.''

Fetterman didn't bother to answer. Instead he got to his feet and headed for the door. Standing in the hallway, looking wet and miserable, were the other members of the team. Fetterman waved them forward. As they approached he said, ''Use the machines and get something good to eat and drink because it might be a while before you have the chance again. Galvin, that man is Sergeant Barlett and he's joining our team. Make sure he doesn't get lost.''

''Sure, Tony. What will you be doing?''

''I want to find our equipment and check it out before they try to palm it off on us. I'll meet you back here as soon as I'm done. Captain'll be down in a few minutes.''

7

UBON AIR FORCE BASE
THAILAND

Fetterman spent nearly an hour checking the equipment, sorting through it all carefully. He examined the parachutes and the reserves, the clothing all dyed black, the boots from West Germany, the Soviet assault rifles that looked almost new, the stacks of ammo and the cartons of C-rations. He searched for signs of rust, tampering, and neglect, but found none.

The combat knives were all brand new, held nearly razor-sharp edges and were dulled to a flat black so they wouldn't catch the sun or reflect the moon. Each of the AKs in the pile had Russian stamping on them, which meant they weren't cheap imitations manufactured in North Vietnam or Red China but quality weapons. It was the best that could be found. Everything looked to be in perfect condition.

He turned, ready to exit the hangar where the equipment was stored, but hesitated. He didn't like leaving it in the open, although access to the area was limited by a security policeman with a roster and a locked door. Fetterman was afraid that someone would sneak in and replace the good stuff with inferior supplies. Once Fetterman and the team parachuted into North Vietnam, who would know the difference.

As he left the hangar he saw Gerber and Tyme coming down the steps from the second floor. He waited until they were close. "Equipment looks good. Checked everything out."

"You meet the Air Force guy?" asked Gerber.

"Yes, sir. We, ah, reached an understanding."

"Uh-huh. He jump qualified?"

"Not by the military but he claims to have been a sky diver, so he's familiar with free-fall. But he probably hasn't made a night jump."

Gerber grinned. "Good. We can scare the shit out of him then."

"Yes, sir."

"And the rest of the team?"

Fetterman looked at Cornett and shrugged. "In the break room having a Coke."

"If you'll have someone watch the door, I'll brief my people in there and then we'll move to the hangar to collect the equipment."

"Fine. And I'll have someone get a deuce and a half into the hangar so you won't get wet on the way to the plane," said Cornett.

"I appreciate that," said Gerber.

"It's to prevent anyone on the base see us moving you from here to the B-52," said Cornett.

They walked from the stairwell until they came to a hallway. Fetterman opened the door of the break room. Gerber stood at the head of the table and looked at his team. Three Special Forces NCOs, an Air Force technician, who didn't look up to a stroll across the airfield, let alone a trip into North Vietnam, and a Vietnamese, a Nung and a woman. Somehow it didn't inspire him with confidence.

"Okay," he said, "here's the deal." He dropped the map on the table, pointed to Ke Sat. "Tomorrow morning we're going to make a HALO infiltration into this area for the purpose of identifying the guidance systems being used on the SAM missiles here."

When the briefing was finished, all of them went to the hangar. Fetterman pawed through the uniforms, finding pieces that would fit the Special Forces men. He found one for Barlett and then they all changed. The Americans were wearing black jungle fatigues with no insignia and no tags. The Vietnamese wore black pajamas and Krung wore tiger-striped fatigues.

Next they divided all the equipment so that everyone would have a load of about equal weight. When the equipment was distributed, Bocker made a radio check, and then they waited for the truck.

Moments later a horn sounded and a yellow light began to flash. An airman who stood at the end of the hangar near the door, pushed a button. The huge doors began to open with a rumble and the breeze, carrying a light mist, swirled in.

Gerber had expected it to be a cold wind because of the thunderstorm that had finally blown itself out, but it wasn't. The mist coated them quickly, and the humidity wouldn't let them dry. Instead of a refreshing evening breeze, they were greeted by an oppressive warmth.

As soon as the door was open far enough, a truck backed in, wrapped in the stench of its diesel engine. It ground to a halt and stood waiting.

"Let's go," said Gerber, shouldering a parachute with one hand and a pack with the other.

Tyme stood still, holding a couple of the AKs by the slings. "This means we're not going to zero the weapons."

"I'm afraid it's a luxury that we don't have time for on this one, Justin."

"Zeroing the weapons is not a luxury, Captain, it's a necessity."

"I understand that, Justin, but there isn't the opportunity to zero the weapons. Besides, we won't be doing any long-range shooting so it's not that critical."

Tyme shook his head and stared at the smooth concrete floor. "I don't like it, sir. I don't like it at all. Maybe once we're on the ground..."

"Once we're on the ground," said Gerber, "we're going to be as quiet as possible. The last thing we need is a bunch of people shooting."

"Yes, sir," said Tyme.

Fetterman approached. "Gear's in the truck."

"Then let's go. Once we're airborne, we can sort it out a little better."

They climbed into the rear of the truck. Gerber crawled along the wooden bench and chose a seat next to the cab. Kit followed, sitting next to him. Krung and Fetterman took positions near the tailgate while the rest of the team got into the other side, working their way around the pile of equipment.

As he sat down Barlett said, "I don't like this."

"You don't have to like it," said Fetterman. "You just have to do it."

"I joined the Air Force to avoid this sort of nonsense," Barlett continued. "If I had wanted to jump into North Vietnam and play in the dark, I would have become a fucking Marine."

"Why don't you shut up?" growled Tyme.

When they were loaded, Cornett dropped the back flap so that no one could see into the truck as it crossed part of the airfield. In the darkened confines of the truck's rear section, Gerber slapped the cab to tell the driver they were ready.

There was a grinding from the front as the starter turned over and then a belch as it caught. The vehicle jerked once, then lurched forward.

As they began to move Kit took Gerber's arm, felt her way down it and clasped his hand. She turned toward him but it was too dark to see, other than an almost invisible silhouette against the black of the cab. She leaned close and whispered, "I'm scared."

Gerber squeezed her hand. "What are you scared about? This is nothing new for you."

"I don't like jumping out of airplanes. And I don't want to go to North Vietnam."

Gerber tried to see the others, but that was impossible in the dark truck. He didn't know if they were listening or not. He whispered, "What scares you about North Vietnam?"

"It truly is my home," Kit answered. "If we are caught, I will be shot as a spy, but not before I'm tortured. They have some people who enjoy that work..."

"Kit, if any of us are caught, we're going to be shot as spies."

"Please do not let them catch me." Her voice was insistent with a note of terror.

"I can't..."

"You *can*," she interrupted. "You can make sure that I am not captured. Please, Captain. As a friend you cannot deny me this one request."

Gerber sat back, forcing himself into the corner between the side of the truck and the cab. With his free hand he wiped the sweat from his face. He needed a breath of fresh air, not the polluted diesel fumes that were blowing into the truck. He felt hot and his stomach was fluttering because he knew what Kit was asking of him. If they got into a situation where they might be captured, she wanted him to kill her. It was something that no one had ever asked of him before and he would refuse to do it, if she hadn't called him a friend.

They were more than that. He knew she loved him, and he had managed to avoid that situation most of the time. She understood his feelings and didn't let that bother her. But beyond that, she was a fellow warrior and a very good one. If that was what she wanted, he was almost honor-bound to grant her request.

He was silent for so long that she thought that he hadn't heard her. "Did you hear me?"

"Yes, I heard." He hesitated before speaking. "No bullshit this time, Kit. You really from North Vietnam?"

"Not far from Ke Sat. A small village on the river. A village called Hung Yen. There they knew my father was French, but they didn't care at first. Then—"

"I'm going to ask you once more, Kit, this the truth? I have to know."

She gripped his hand tighter. "Yes. This time it's the truth. I told those other stories because I thought that was what your interrogators wanted to hear. I told them all what they wanted to hear. I made up some good stories, too, but this time I'm telling you the truth."

"Okay, Kit. I'll make sure you aren't captured." But even as he said it, he wasn't sure he could do it. Fetterman could. Fetterman seemed to understand these things on a level that was below the conscious mind. He understood that sometimes the greatest gift you could give to a friend was death. Gerber knew it, too, but wasn't sure he had the courage to do it.

If he told Fetterman of the request, Fetterman would offer to carry it out, but this was something that Gerber couldn't delegate. It was something he'd have to do himself.

"I'll make sure," he repeated and then resolved to keep that situation from happening.

There was a squeal of brakes and the rocking of the truck stopped. Fetterman threw the flap up and out of the way, then disappeared over the top of the tailgate. Gerber could see the soft blue lights of the airfield's taxiways. Standing there was the B-52, a black shape that rumbled and vibrated as the crew prepared it for flight.

"Come on, people," said Fetterman. "We haven't got all night. Let's get the gear loaded."

Gerber slid along the bench, following Kit. He dropped to the ground as one of the people from the aircraft approached. Over the sound of the engines, or the APUs, Gerber wasn't sure which, the man shouted, "Who's Gerber?"

"I'm Captain Gerber."

"I'm Major Martin," said the man.

In the dark, Gerber couldn't tell much about him except that he seemed to be short and skinny. His voice was deep, though.

"I'm not accustomed to carrying passengers, especially ones who will be leaving early."

"Not my idea, either," said Gerber.

"As soon as your men get their gear stowed on board we can get this wound up." He shook his head. "I don't know how you're going to do it."

"Thought we'd go out the bomb bay," said Gerber.

"Yeah," said Martin, as if he wasn't sure about that, either.

Fetterman joined them, "Sir, there are a couple of questions I need to ask and no one I talked to had the answers for. First, is it possible for us to bail out the bomb bay?"

"I wouldn't think that would be a problem." Martin hesitated before adding, "Probably not the best way to get out of a plane, but it's all I can suggest."

"Okay. We need to have you slow to your lowest airspeed so you don't scatter us all over the place and we need to all get out as quickly as possible."

Martin looked around. "I'm not sure how we're going to do this." He rubbed a hand on the back of his neck. "I suppose I'll reduce the speed, open the bomb bay and out you go. Why don't you get your equipment over to the hatch there and the crew will get it stored for takeoff."

"You've been briefed?" asked Gerber.

"I know what's supposed to happen."

"Going out the bomb bay, we'll need a place to hook the static lines of the equipment pods," said Fetterman.

"Get with the crew chief," said Martin. "There's some handholds in there that might work for you."

"Yes, sir," said Fetterman. "I'll want to get a look at the bomb bay and check it out. Something that should have been done before anyone sent us out here."

A yellow truck with headlights blazing and a flashing light on the roof of its cab stopped near the front of the giant bomber. It sat there for a moment and through the back window they could see the driver twisted around looking at them.

"We're almost ready for takeoff," said Martin.

Fetterman turned and waved a hand. "Grab the gear."

Another Air Force officer appeared and pointed, "Use that hatch there. Spread it out along the bulkheads so that we don't have all the weight concentrated in one spot."

Fetterman moved off to supervise the loading of the equipment. He helped Kit pick up a bundle and together they carried it to the hatch. They hoisted it, and a man there snagged it and dragged it inside. In a few minutes they had the equipment loaded and were handing up the weapons, none of which were loaded.

Martin saw the progress and watched as first Kit, and then the rest of the team, disappeared into the belly of the aircraft. Martin touched Gerber on the shoulder. "Let's go."

Inside, Gerber found that his team was scattered throughout the plane, taking the seats that had been added for inspectors. Belted in and waiting, none of them looked thrilled by the idea of riding in the rear of a B-52, unable to see out and having to trust their fate to Air Force pilots who didn't look old enough to have graduated from high school, let alone find time to learn to fly.

Gerber strapped himself into a chair near the navigator. He tossed a glance over his shoulder and saw Kit sitting with her eyes closed and clutching the arms of her chair.

The engine noise increased as each of the ten engines was started. Gerber sat quietly watching the flashing lights on the panel in front of him, occasionally shooting a glance out the window nearby. He couldn't see much, just light reflecting off the low cloud base that had spawned the thunderstorm earlier.

They started to move with a gentle tug. The aircraft vibrated as they rolled along the taxiway and took up their position on the runway. A moment later the roar of the engines built into a thunder that wiped away all other sound. The vibrations increased until it seemed the plane would shake itself apart, and then they were racing down the runway and finally clawing their way into the sky.

For the first few minutes Gerber was forced back into his seat by the pressure of the climb. He sat there quietly as the aircraft shuddered in the turbulence, telling himself over and over that the pilot would never have taken off if the weather was too bad and that the jolting and rattling were normal.

They leveled out and everyone seemed to relax. The navigator looked at Gerber. "You planning to bail out at thirty thousand feet?"

"Yes. Why?"

"You know a person remains conscious for only seconds unless you're on oxygen."

"Of course."

"And you know that the air temperature is something like thirty or forty degrees below zero."

"Is there a point to all this?" asked Gerber.

"I just wondered if you've done anything like this before."

"Never out of the belly of a bomber, but I have made high-altitude jumps. We've got some gear to keep us warm and some disposable oxygen bottles."

"Oh." He was silent for a moment and then said, "You're going out in the dark. How can you do that?"

Gerber smiled. "Simple. We've got an altimeter on top of the reserve. Besides, you can see the horizon. There's plenty of light to see by."

The navigator shook his head. "Christ, what a deal."

The flight into North Vietnam was short. Within what seemed like minutes, the copilot came back and said, "We'll be in position in about ten minutes."

"Thanks." Gerber unbuckled his seat belt and flipped the shoulder harness out of the way. He stood, ducking his head to keep from hitting it on the low-hanging beams, then moved toward the rear to find Fetterman. He signaled the master sergeant and they all moved to the hatch that led into the bomb bay.

Together they gathered their team at the hatch. They helped one another into their parachutes, checking each other. Tyme passed out the weapons, handing each of them a magazine that he had loaded himself. He still wasn't happy about not having time to zero them, but that couldn't be helped now.

When everyone was set, Fetterman checked them one final time. Gerber stood next to Kit. "You know how to use this?" He pointed to the altimeter and the oxygen bottle attached to her equipment.

"Yes."

"Okay. Once we're outside you'll be able to see this. When the little hand rolls down to the glowing line, you'll be about a thousand feet above the ground. Pull the rip cord."

"I understand."

One of the crewmen came back. "Pilot wants to depressurize. You'll have to go to oxygen. Be about three minutes after that."

"Put on your oxygen masks," instructed Gerber. He tucked the bottle under the straps of his parachute harness, then tugged a ski mask over his face to protect it from the biting cold of the upper atmosphere. He rolled down the sleeves of his uniform, then pulled on a jacket and the gloves that would protect his hands. When he finished, he looked at his team, found them ready, and held a thumbs-up. One of the crewmen used the intercom to alert the pilot.

After the depressurization was completed, Fetterman opened the hatch into the bomb bay. The doors in the belly of the plane were closed and it was nearly pitch black in there. A moment later a light came on and Fetterman stepped through. Using the static lines, he attached the rip cords of the equipment pods to the handholds. Next he arranged the team the way he wanted them to bail out, pointing to each of them. He could feel the cold of the atmosphere seeping into the belly of the bomber. In seconds his toes began to tingle.

The crewman stuck his head in. "When the lights go out, it'll mean the pilot is going to open the bomb bay."

Fetterman held up a thumb to indicate that he understood the instructions.

Over the roar Gerber shouted, "We've got to get out quickly. Even at the reduced speed, if we hesitate, we're going to be scattered over several miles and won't be able to regroup."

At that moment the lights went out.

"Remember. Out quickly."

As Fetterman stepped back, there was a whine of servo motors and the bomb bay opened so that there was a rectangle of gray. The roar of the wind and engines filled the interior of the plane as bitterly cold wind swirled in, buffeting them.

The crewman who had remained near them shouted, "Thirty seconds. Twenty. Ten..."

Fetterman shifted around so that he could dump the equipment pods. As soon as they were clear, Tyme would jump, followed by Gerber, Barlett, Kit, Krung, Duc and then Bocker. If they weren't all out in seconds, they would be widely scattered.

The crewman counted down the seconds and as he shouted "One!", Fetterman shoved the pods. As they tumbled clear, Tyme plunged into space. Gerber was just a gray blur as he dived through the bomb bay. Barlett went out like an expert. Kit hesitated for an instant and Fetterman thought he was going to have to push her. Then she was out, looking like a teenager jumping into the cold water of the neighborhood swimming pool.

As soon as the others had jumped, Fetterman flashed a thumbs-up at the crewman who now stood in the hatch, and dived through the opening. He stretched out in a spread-eagle position to stabilize his descent. Below him, he could see the dark shapes of two of the men and the dark smears that marked the canopies of the equipment pods.

He turned in time to see the three planes in the B-52 flight disappearing from sight, blue-white flames marking the engine pods. Then, on the ground below them were orange-yellow flashes as the bombs from two of them exploded. Another diversion.

From miles away, he saw the muzzle flashes of the anti-aircraft weapons. There were air bursts, but nothing that came close to the B-52s as they turned toward the east, heading for their base in Guam.

He looked down and watched the numbers on the altimeter unwinding rapidly. In front of him was the line of the horizon, a sharp, defined line, easily visible. There was the black of the ground and the dark gray of the night sky. From the angle, Fetterman could tell that he was close to a thousand feet.

He glanced at the altimeter a last time and pulled the rip cord. He felt the chute pull free and heard the whispering sound behind him as the canopy spilled from his pack. There was a single, soft jerk and then a harder one that yanked the harness tight against his crotch.

Seconds later he watched the ground come up to meet his feet and he rolled to his shoulder in a perfect PLF. The ground was soft and damp and cold. He came to his feet and punched at the harness release so that the billowing chute wouldn't drag him across the open ground. Then he moved along the risers, rolling the chute into a loose ball. Finally, he determined a westerly course, where he hoped to find the others, and started walking.

8

THE FIELDS SOUTH OF
KE SAT NORTH VIETNAM

Gerber hit the ground hard, rolled into a muddy hole and then scrambled to his feet. He punched the quick release on the chute harness and stripped the oxygen mask from his face. He wiped the back of his hand across his face and realized that he was still wearing the ski mask. Instead of whipping it off, he left it on, using the black material to hide his features from the bright moonlight.

Free of the chute, he crouched on one knee, and felt the cold water seep through the fabric of his uniform. He let his eyes roam the open fields for signs of people moving, of soldiers maneuvering, but saw nothing. He gathered up his chute, rolled it into a soggy, loose ball and then started moving toward the north and the rally point.

At the edge of a tree line—he couldn't tell if it was the jungle or forest—he stopped and listened. Cautiously, he moved into it, staying near the edge so he would see anyone coming toward him. He dropped his chute and quietly worked a round into the chamber of his AK-47. Then he waited, his breath rasping in his throat, wishing that he had a drink. He knew he wasn't thirsty, and that the desire was a psychological effect of the jump and the situation, but that didn't lessen the desire for water. He fought off the urge and kept his eyes on the open ground in front of him.

After several minutes he caught a flicker of movement. He turned toward it and lost it and then looked away. With his peripheral vision, he found it again and watched as the man-sized shape worked its way toward the trees. Gerber didn't feel the need to challenge the man. He recognized the form and the hat and the weapon. Tyme stopped just inside the trees, and let the chute he carried fall to the ground.

Gerber hissed at him, saw him spin at the noise and then grin, his teeth white in the black of the night. He slipped closer to Gerber, dropped to one knee, and put his lips close to Gerber's ears.

"Didn't see any of the others."

"Damn," said Gerber. "I was afraid we'd scatter all over hell and gone."

A voice came from their right. "I'd suggest you two hold it down."

Gerber dropped to his stomach, aiming at the sound, before he recognized the voice as Fetterman's. Feeling foolish, he got up and moved deeper into the trees.

"As you can see," said Fetterman, "I managed to locate Kit, Krung and Galvin while you two played footsie."

"You didn't see either Barlett or Duc?"

"Nope. Did find the equipment pods, though, and managed to get them over here."

"Good," said Gerber. He reached up and pulled the ski mask off his face. There was a rush of cold air that made him shiver. He mopped the sweat from his forehead with the mask, stuffed it into a pocket. He turned to Tyme, "Get this stuff buried. Doesn't have to be too deep or too good because we aren't going to be around that long."

"What about the others?" asked Fetterman. "How long do we wait for them?"

Gerber pulled the camouflage cover from the luminous dial of his watch. "I make it an hour, hour and a half to sunrise. Take us thirty minutes to bury the equipment. They have thirty minutes."

"You going to leave them, then?" asked Fetterman.

"I don't see that I have any choice. We can't hang around here, and I don't want to leave anyone else behind. They know the target, so if they're in the clear they know where to go."

"That's what bothers me," said Fetterman. "Both know where we're going and I don't think it would take much for the North Vietnamese to convince Barlett to tell all he knows. All they have to do is suggest they're going to beat him, and he'll open up."

Gerber wiped his face again. "We can be in place tomorrow night. I can't see how he could compromise us that quickly even if he tries."

"Unless he walks into one of their patrols and starts talking the second they catch him."

"We can't abort now, Master Sergeant," said Gerber. "You want to stay here and wait for them?"

"No, sir, but I will. I think I should give them until midmorning at the latest. Besides, it'll give me a chance to clean up the DZ and spot their bodies in case they were killed in the jump."

"If they're dead, they're no problem."

"Yes, sir. Unless the bodies are recognized as parachutists and not pilots who bailed out. I'll hide them if I find them. I'll wait."

"Okay. The rest of us are getting the hell out of here." He dropped to one knee and pulled his compass from one of his pockets. He sighted a course to the north and pointed it out to Bocker.

"You sure we're in the right DZ?" asked Bocker when Gerber told him to take the point.

"No, and I won't be until it's light enough to see a couple of landmarks. Until that time, I want you to head zero-two-zero degrees and stop when you come to anything big."

"Yes, sir."

Gerber organized them quickly, telling Tyme to bring up the rear. Bocker then slipped deeper into the trees, followed by Krung and Kit. Gerber was right behind her, one hand on her shoulder as they stepped out. He then dropped back a pace so that he could barely see her outline as they moved among the shadows of the forest.

Bocker set a rapid pace because the vegetation was very light, more like a forest with very little undergrowth than the tangled nightmares of the South. There wasn't a canopy overhead so that moonlight and starlight filtered through, giving them enough illumination to see. Bocker avoided the big trees and bushes, using a branch as a walking stick to test the ground in front of him. The last thing he wanted to do was walk off a cliff or drop into a hole.

After an hour, Gerber noticed that it was getting brighter. Trees and bushes that had been little more than dark outlines against a gray background were beginning to take on detail. There were occasional flashes of movement as small animals and lizards scurried through the forest. The sky had paled and some of the stars had faded. As he saw that, he moved forward, passing Kit and Krung, until he caught Bocker. He stopped him and the patrol scattered among the ferns, trees and vegetation.

"I think we need to find a hiding place for the morning," said Gerber.

Five minutes later Bocker found the perfect spot. There was a source of water close by and good cover. They fanned out, with Bocker working his way into the clump of bushes and brush, leading them in. Once everyone except Gerber was inside and hidden, the Special Forces captain checked the ground around them for signs that they had been there. He found a couple of footprints that were rapidly filling with water and located a dozen others that had been made by the locals. There was nothing that pointed to them.

He slipped into the cover, being careful not to bend and snap the tiniest branches of the small bush or crush the newest blades of grass. While Bocker and Tyme took the first guard rotation, Gerber ate some cold C-rations. These had been packaged by the West Germans for the NATO forces, so it was doubtful that it would fool the North Vietnamese about who was there and using them, but it certainly wouldn't point directly at the Americans.

Gerber ate the food rapidly, buried the remains at the base of a small bush, and then drank part of his water. He set the canteen on the ground next to him and rolled over so that he was almost wrapped around the bush. The low-hanging branches concealed him.

Moments later he felt a light pressure along his spine. He turned his head and saw that Kit had crawled into the bush with him. She was now clinging to his back, molding herself to him.

Gerber whispered. "We've got to spread out."

"No one will see us."

"For safety. We can't all clump up like this."

"I feel safe this way," she said. She slid forward and nuzzled the back of his neck and then breathed into his ear. "I feel very safe."

"Kit, we've got to spread out."

She didn't move except to lick his ear. Gerber felt shivers up and down his spine. He wanted to shout at her, shove her away from him, but couldn't. It would make too much noise. Besides, he could see too well. The sun was up, lighting the whole forest, and the bigger animals were beginning to stir. In minutes the local population would be out of their hootches heading to work in the nearby fields. He couldn't afford noise or movement.

"If you insist," he hissed, "you can stay, but behave yourself. Get some sleep."

She didn't answer, but she did stop working on his ear. He felt her face on the back of his neck and then felt the slow, moist exhalations on his bare skin there. She wrapped one arm over him, holding him tightly.

FETTERMAN MADE A QUICK, quiet search of the DZ but had no luck locating either Duc or Barlett. As the sun came up he slipped to the north and found a hiding place in the trees. He waited patiently, scanning the ground, searching for a sign of either the airdrop or the fate of Barlett or Duc. But there was nothing.

To the east he heard a babble of voices and then a lone man wearing black pajamas walked into the field. He turned once and shouted something to whoever was hidden in the trees there. Then he continued across the open field. About halfway to the other side he stopped, staring at the ground. He cocked his head to the right, looked around, then stooped over. He plucked something out of the mud, turned his back to Fetterman and examined whatever it was.

The man stood and put one hand to his forehead to shield his eyes from the rays of the rising sun. He looked toward the woods and it was then that Fetterman saw what he held in his hand. An Air Force combat knife like the one Barlett had worn the night before. Although it was more a survival tool than a fighting knife, it wasn't something that Fetterman wanted swung at him. As the man started toward him, Fetterman climbed from his belly to his hands and knees and then to his feet. Crouching so that he was covered by the dying branches of a fallen tree, Fetterman slipped to the right.

The man looked at the forest where Fetterman crouched, almost as if he had seen the Special Forces sergeant. He took a step forward, looked over his shoulder and then started to walk again. At the edge of the trees he hesitated and then plunged in. He shoved a branch to the side and stopped.

When it seemed that the man was momentarily distracted by something in the forest, Fetterman moved toward him with catlike agility despite the weight of the equipment he wore. He clapped a hand over the North Vietnamese's nose and mouth and shoved the blade of the West German combat knife up through the man's kidney and into his left lung. Then, as he pulled the man backward, he withdrew the knife and dragged it across the throat, severing the larynx from the trachea and cutting both the carotid arteries. A warm flow of blood ran down the man's chest as he died. A foul stench assaulted Fetterman's nostrils.

Fetterman ignored both the sticky, coppery-smelling blood, and the odor of bowel, dragging the man deeper into the trees. He hadn't wanted to kill him, but the man held Barlett's knife and Fetterman was afraid that it would be enough to compromise the mission. A smart enemy officer might figure it out.

He rolled the man over and stared at the face, now waxy looking. The eyes were open and unfocused. Fetterman pried the knife from the death grip of the man and then quickly searched him. In South Vietnam the man would have been suspicious because he was a "military-age male," but in the North, Fetterman wasn't sure that the term applied. Still, he had no choice.

He found a pistol concealed under the black silk shirt. That could only mean the man was an officer in some military unit. This wasn't a weapon captured from the French, but a Soviet-made 9 mm Makarov. Fetterman took the weapon and shoved it into his waistband.

Now Fetterman was certain that the man hadn't been a harmless peasant out for a morning walk, but an officer, possibly searching for the parachutists who had dropped the night before. Maybe a farmer had seen something and reported it. Not enough for the man to initiate a full-blown search, but enough so that he decided to come out to look around for himself.

After Fetterman concealed the body, he hoped the dead man wouldn't be missed for a couple of days. A minor official might not be missed for a week. There was no telling. It all depended on what he had shouted at the men who had remained hidden in the trees.

Fetterman worked his way back to the edge of the forest and peered into the open area. He waited quietly for fifteen minutes, but the only sounds were those made by the animals and the insects. And although the sun had barely cleared the horizon, it was already hot and humid. Sweat from the exertion of the fight didn't evaporate, but dripped along his sides, tickling him. It ran down his face and stung his eyes. But Fetterman didn't move, waiting for the ambush to spring, and waiting for the men to appear in the trees, but nothing happened.

When it was clear that no one had followed the man, and obvious that neither Duc nor Barlett was going to turn up, Fetterman crawled to the rear. When he was thirty or forty meters into the forest, he got to his feet. There was a rough trail leading to the north, a path worn deep by the feet of hundreds of North Vietnamese. The vines hanging from the trees, the lacy leaves of the ferns and the broad-leafed branches of bushes had been trimmed back so that they didn't block the trail. It looked like a green tunnel through the forest. Naturally, Fetterman avoided it.

Instead he worked his way through the trees, moving quickly and silently, slipping around the obstacles. He didn't want to touch anything, afraid that he would leave signs that an astute tracker could read. That slowed his progress, and it wasn't until midmorning that he reached the area where Gerber had taken refuge for the day.

IT TOOK MOST OF THE MORNING for George and Robin to track down Jerry Maxwell. At first he had been out of the office, and each time they checked somewhere, they were told that he had just left. Finally they had caught up to him at MACV Headquarters. The MP at the iron gate wouldn't let them through until Maxwell came out of his office to vouch for them. Then, reluctantly, he let them through, cautioning them not to go anywhere without Maxwell and not to poke their heads into any of the other offices.

Maxwell opened the door for them and let them enter the cold, dim interior of his office. He hit the light switch. "Forgive the clutter, but I've been busy lately. Grab a seat where you can."

Robin entered and fell into the large visitor's chair. She watched George move to the rear near the file cabinets. She leaned to the right, an elbow on the desk, glancing at the labels on the folders that were stamped Secret.

"What can I do for you now?" asked Maxwell, taking the seat in front of the desk. Nonchalantly, he tried to slip the Secret material into the drawer away from Robin.

"I'm not sure that I know how you can help," said George, leaning against the files.

Robin crossed her legs slowly, letting the hem of her skirt ride up. She wanted to smile as she saw Maxwell staring at her legs.

He tore his eyes away and shot a glance at George. "Why don't you just tell me what you want?"

George made a production of pulling a notebook from the pocket of his sweat-stained khaki safari shirt. "We know that Gerber and Fetterman have taken off on some kind of important hush-hush mission."

"So?" said Maxwell, turning. He noticed that the top two buttons on Robin's blouse were open. As he shifted to his left slightly, he could see down her blouse to the gentle swell of her breasts and the white lacy cup of her bra.

"So?" he repeated, distracted by Robin.

"So, we know that Gerber is out of the country."

Maxwell jerked around. "There is no way you could know that."

"Given what we know, we believe he is in North Vietnam," said George.

"Jerry," said Robin quickly, "we don't want you to violate any of your rules on secrecy, but we do want the story. We want it exclusively, as soon as it can be released without jeopardizing the men involved." Casually she reached down, scratched her leg and managed to pull the hem of her skirt even higher.

Maxwell kept his eyes on the pile of paper on his desk and then on the ceiling and finally on the wall about six inches above Robin's head. When he thought she wasn't watching, he looked at her legs.

"There isn't much to tell," said Maxwell.

"Come on, Jerry," said Robin. "I know better than that. Mack was supposed to have dinner with me last night. He left the room in the morning and never even called. That means something big came up.''

"Damn," said Maxwell, and then tried to recover. "All it means is that he was sent out to check on the possibility of a Montagnard revolt."

"Wait a minute," snapped George. "What in hell are you talking about?"

Maxwell realized that his attempted cover story had blown up the moment he had pulled it. Inside MACV, he had been instructed to hint at a Montagnard revolt in some of the strike companies if someone missed Gerber or Fetterman, or had a suspicion that something was going on. Outside, he should have just denied everything.

"Robin, George, please. We're treading on ground here that is very shaky. I'm not sure what you should know, but too much of this getting out could be damaging to the war effort and prove dangerous to some of our people."

"You know," said George as he scribbled in his notebook, "I'm getting a little tired of that old chestnut. Every time you clowns make a mistake, let too much information slip, you fall back to national security or the war effort. It's beginning to wear thin."

"Sometimes it's true," said Maxwell. "Too much out now could get people killed."

Robin leaned across the desk and patted Maxwell's arm. "We're not out to hurt anyone," she said. "We just want to know what in the hell is going on."

Maxwell turned back to her and looked down her blouse. He could almost see her navel, but her breasts and nipples were discreetly covered by her bra. Maxwell found the peek-a-boo game to be very stimulating. He didn't want to do anything to end it, yet he didn't want to tell them things they had no need, no right to know.

As a compromise he said, "You forget that about the Montagnards and I'll give you something else. Tell you a little about what Mack Gerber is doing now."

"I'll go along with that," said Robin, rocking back in the chair.

"As long as it's good," said George. "We reserve the right to refuse if it becomes clear that you're handing us a line of shit."

"Okay," said Maxwell, realizing that he had dug himself a deep hole. "Mack Gerber, Sergeant Fetterman, and a small group of Special Forces NCOs are on a trail-watching mission just inside the Cambodian border."

"Oh, Christ," said George.

"Now wait a minute," said Maxwell, holding up a hand. "They're looking for evidence of a massive buildup of enemy forces in this region, including the influx of heavy weapons, like 20 mm and 37 mm antiaircraft weapons."

George shook his head. "Not going to wash, Jerry. That's not nearly as good as a revolt in the strike companies. And you've been using that one for too long."

"I never said there would be a revolt, but publishing a story like that could precipitate one. We just know that some of the Montagnards are unhappy. Our people are working to head it off, but too much information now could foil their attempts and jeopardize some of our people."

"How is that, Jerry? The Montagnards read the American newspapers?" asked George.

"I'm just saying that such a report would be, ah, premature."

"You're talking awfully fast," said Robin. She smiled at him and lowered her eyelids, trying to look sexy.

Maxwell studied her for a moment. She was showing him the long expanse of her leg and quite a bit of her thigh. She kept tugging ineffectually at the hem of her skirt. Suddenly he realized that he was being double-teamed. Her job was to distract him while George fed him the hard questions. He felt sick to his stomach as he realized how easily they had done it to him.

"I'm not going to tell you anything else. Just get out of here. You print anything and I'll call it a lie. I'll see that your press credentials are revoked and that you're both expelled from Vietnam."

"What's this?" asked Robin.

"Just get out," repeated Maxwell. He wanted to say that he had thought they were friends, maybe a little more than friends, but she had violated that. She had changed the rules of the game so that she was using his affection for her against him. She had been leading him along, flirting with him so that he would give out more than he should.

And he had fallen for it like a college boy new to the agency. Fallen for a pretty woman flashing some thigh and letting him look down her blouse. And it wasn't as if she had shown him anything. It made him angry that she would try something like that. And it made him angry that he had been dumb enough to fall for it.

At least he hadn't told them anything they didn't already know. Somehow they had learned that Gerber was off on a mission, but they had no idea of what or where. While they chased around the camps near the Cambodian and Laotian borders, Gerber would be finishing his mission in the North and then it would be too late to do any damage.

Robin watched Maxwell for a moment and then stood, smoothing her skirt over her thighs. It stopped a few inches short of her knees.

Without a word, they left the office. As they approached the iron gate they heard the door slam, but neither looked back. They checked out, walked upstairs and then out into the almost unbearable heat of late morning.

As he blinked in the sun, George said, "He gave us more than he thought he did."

Robin shook her head. "I don't feel good about what we did."

"What's not to feel good about? We went in, used the little information we had to get some more. We now know that Gerber is in North Vietnam and Fetterman is with him. We know that they have a team in there and we know that there might be a Montagnard revolt. Hell, this could keep us busy for a month and get us a Pulitzer prize."

Robin put a hand up to shade her eyes. She felt the sweat bead on her forehead, under her arms and drip between her breasts. "I don't feel good about using my friendship with Jerry Maxwell the way I did. I was flirting with him to get information."

"If you feel that strongly, ask him out to dinner. Hold his hand, kiss. Hell, fuck him if it'll make you feel better."

"George, sometimes you're a real horse's ass." She looked at him and then added, "Not sometimes. All the time."

He touched her shoulder. "That may be true, my girl, but I'm one hell of a reporter."

9

SOMEWHERE NEAR KE SAT NORTH VIETNAM

Gerber snapped awake, sweating in the heat of the early afternoon, his black uniform soaked with perspiration. The fact that Kit still clung to his back didn't help matters, and the bush that kept the direct rays of the sun off him trapped the humid air around him. It felt as if someone had dumped a bucket of warm water over him.

For a moment he lay still, quietly listening to the sounds around him. The buzz of insects, the scratching of tiny claws as small animals climbed through the center of the bush, and the calling of birds as they screamed at one another. There was a crashing overhead as a couple of monkeys played in the treetops. He opened his eyes and stared at the rough, thorny bark of the trunk. He didn't want to move and wake Kit and then realized that she was awake.

He pushed backward and felt her shift out of the way. As he crawled from under the bush he listened for sounds of people other than his team. To the left he saw a large black shape that had to be Sergeant Bocker hiding. In the other direction, Sergeant Tyme watched the open ground that led to the clump of trees and bushes where they hid.

While Kit crawled deeper into the bush, Gerber slipped the map from his damp pocket. The map had been printed on thin vinyl to withstand the moisture of the tropics. He unfolded it carefully, and then refolded it so that the patch of North Vietnam where he was supposed to be was on top. Using his compass, he sighted on the landmarks he could see. Once he crawled to the edge of the forest and found a thin, broken streambed that sparkled in the sunlight. He took a compass reading. In the distance, to the northwest, he could hear the occasional rumble of a truck, indicating a road. And there was a swampy area to the southwest. Given all that, he was sure that the Air Force had dropped him right where they had said they would—south of Ke Sat.

With the compass and the map, he figured out a route that would get him to the SAM complex near Ke Sat after dark. It was through light forest and scrub, and barring unforeseen incidents like an American bombing mission, which he had been promised would not go in, or NVA maneuvers, they could get there a little after midnight.

Convinced that he knew exactly where they were, Gerber crawled to Tyme. He touched the young sergeant on the shoulder and pointed to the rear. Before Tyme could move, Gerber leaned close. "Fetterman?"

Tyme shook his head and shrugged. "You want me to look for him?"

Gerber shook his head, then folded his hands and placed them against his head as if he was sleeping. He also motioned to his mouth as if he was eating. He was telling Tyme to get some sleep or to eat something. To take it easy. And that they shouldn't be talking, given the circumstances.

Tyme's face was stained with camouflage paint, which made him look like a green-black nightmare vision in a horror film. He grinned, showing perfect white teeth. He nodded his understanding and worked his way into the trees and bushes, disappearing from sight in seconds. Although Gerber listened intently, he could not hear Tyme moving. There was only the quietest rustling of the bushes, caused by the light breeze.

For nearly an hour Gerber lay there motionless, his eyes shifting right and left as he watched for the NVA and the local civilian population. His left elbow was in a puddle of water, but it wasn't an unpleasant sensation. He could feel water seeping through his clothes to mingle with his sweat. Through the lacy curtain of an overhanging fern, he could watch a trail, and to the right, he could see a clearing carpeted with short grass and wild flowers.

A rustling to his left caught his attention. Kit appeared and crawled to him. She didn't speak. She put her lips next to his ear, as if she wanted to talk, but then blew her hot breath on him.

His first reaction was annoyance because it wasn't the time or place for games and then he realized that it was the time and place. Maybe the only time and place they would have for the next forty-eight or seventy-two hours. Instead of reprimanding her, he glanced at her and grinned, but didn't respond. After a couple of minutes she stopped, withdrawing to the hideout.

An hour later, Krung relieved him. Gerber crawled to the rear for water and food and to plan for the night mission. He found Kit sitting with her back to a tree trunk, her black pajama trousers pulled up to expose her legs to the light breeze. She had unbuttoned her blouse, letting it hang open. When she moved, he could see her small breasts.

He wanted to laugh. That was the last thing they needed on a patrol. A little sex to lighten the mood. He crawled past her and sat facing the other direction so that he wouldn't have to look at her. Besides, it made good sense. Cover all the approaches.

As the light began to fade, Gerber pulled Bocker to the side and whispered to him. "I'll want you on point again tonight. I don't think Tony is going to find us before we have to move out of here."

"Shouldn't we look for him?"

"Why?" Gerber wanted to laugh. The idea that Fetterman was lost was ridiculous. He had thought that Fetterman would find them before dusk. But now Gerber expected to find him at the SAM site. He said as much to Bocker and then added, "I think Kit should be right behind you, so she can help. According to her, this is her homeland. I don't know if it is or not, but if she has a suggestion, listen to it."

"Do I take it?" asked Bocker.

"Shit, I don't know. Let the situation dictate. If you think she's slinging crap, ignore her."

Bocker wiped his mouth with the back of his hand. "Do we—do you—trust her?"

Gerber sighed and looked around toward her. He saw the swell of her calf and trim ankle. He thought of everything they had been through together, thought of the hillside in Cambodia and the opportunities she'd had to betray them. "Yeah, Galvin, I think I do. But keep on your toes."

"Yes, sir. When do we move out?"

Gerber pulled back the camouflage cover of his watch. "Thirty minutes, moving slow and easy." Gerber showed him the map, the compass headings, and the major landmarks. He was going to explain how to go about navigating in the dark, then remembered that Bocker was on his second tour of duty, too. If he couldn't read a compass and navigate at night in unfamiliar territory, he had no business in Special Forces or in Vietnam.

With Bocker briefed, Gerber circled the tiny perimeter, talking to each of the men with him. He detailed Tyme for the rear guard and told Krung to hang back, close to Tyme, in case the young sergeant needed help. Both Tyme and Krung asked about leaving Fetterman behind and Gerber told them the same thing he had told Bocker.

Finally they shouldered the equipment, checking it to make sure that it was still in good condition or that it hadn't gotten wet during the day, and that there was nothing on it to rattle. Before he signaled Bocker forward, Gerber finished the water in one of his canteens so it wouldn't slosh around as they maneuvered in the forest.

With that, they moved out, leaving the campsite. Tyme would hesitate there for a moment and clean up anything they might have left behind. Their progress was rapid while they still had some light. The group moved through a forest that had little in the way of undergrowth. There were saplings and tiny trees all around them, and a carpet of dead leaves that was decaying so quickly it was a moist, slimy film and not a brittle, crackling booby trap.

When the sun set, the forest didn't turn into the black morass that the jungle did in the South. There was still light, from the moon, from the stars, from the fluorescent decaying vegetation. There were shades of gray and streaks of black with pale areas and ribbons of silver. There were sharp contrasts between the trees and the bushes and open ground. Bocker seemed to have a knack for choosing the path of least resistance and they made good time.

Once or twice they heard the scream of jet engines from passing aircraft, and once, in the distance, the crump of antiaircraft fire. The cry of a large cat slowed them for a few minutes. Gerber hadn't been frightened by the animal, but afraid they would find it necessary to shoot it. Of course, in North Vietnam, many farmers were armed with automatic weapons and were told to shoot at any American planes they saw. Pilots had reported seeing the tracers from those farmers on dozens of occasions. Still there was no point in advertising their presence.

They stopped to rest a couple of times, the men and Kit spreading out in a loose circle so that they would have a view of the entire area around them. Gerber wanted to drink his water. His mouth felt as if it was filled with cotton from the exertion of the night march through the forest. But he didn't want to drain a second canteen, sure that if he did, he would need the water later.

After ten minutes, they were up and moving again. Bocker, Kit, Gerber and then Krung and Tyme. They wormed their way through the forest and out onto an open field. Crouching they hurried across it and then came to a road. Since there was no traffic, Bocker didn't even stop. He sprinted to the other side and disappeared into the woods. When there was no firing, the rest of them hurried to the other side.

Thirty minutes later Bocker dropped to the ground at the edge of the trees. Gerber crawled to him. There was a four-foot-high earthen breastwork about fifty yards in front of him. Sticking up above it was the nose of a missile that was pointed more or less toward the sky. There seemed to be no one moving anywhere near the missile.

"Captain?" asked Bocker.

Gerber studied the moon and stars, figuring it was about midnight. They were supposed to listen for instructions on the radio if they were in a position to do so, but the last thing Gerber wanted to do was break out the radio equipment. There would be more instructions at six.

"We watch for a while."

"And then?"

"We penetrate the missile site and see if you can make heads or tails of the guidance system."

Bocker nodded, the gesture lost in the darkness. "I was afraid you'd say something like that."

NEARLY HALF A KLICK AWAY, Master Sergeant Anthony B. Fetterman crouched under the leaves of a flowering bush and examined the tail fins of a different SA-2 Guideline missile. He was no more than fifty meters from the missile, hidden on a slight ridge that allowed him to look down on it. The earthwork berm that protected the weapon didn't conceal it from him. Even part of the concrete road and the hardstand were visible in the pale moonlight.

As Fetterman studied the weapon he thought there was something wrong with it. It somehow didn't look right. The missile itself, a two-stage rocket with four tail fins, a set of small stabilizing fins about a third of the way forward and then a final, larger set just in front of that, seemed to be real enough.

It was the launcher that wasn't right. Fetterman knew that the SA-2 rested on a metal turret that could be rotated as first the Spoon Rest and then the Fan Song radars acquired and tracked targets. Hydraulics in the metallic base raised and lowered the missile, depending on the range and altitude of the incoming enemy jets. Behind the missile was a thick metal blast plate to protect the site.

Even in the moonlight the whole firing platform looked phony. It seemed to be no more than a training mock-up, to be used by the NVA for their recruits. From the air, it would resemble a real SAM site, especially in a jet traveling at five or six hundred miles an hour.

As a lone cloud slipped in front of the moon, Fetterman crept from his hiding place, and slid down the hillside until his feet rested at the base of a dry rice paddy dike. He crawled over it and then got to his feet. Crouching, he ran along the side of the dike, leaped over another, then dropped to the ground.

Around him, he heard nothing except the night sounds of the rice paddies. Insects buzzing in search of food. A light breeze rustled the grass growing on the dikes. From the missile complex there was nothing.

He felt sweat dripping down his temple but ignored it. Instead he scrambled to the side, up and over the dike and crawled along it until he reached a corner of the paddy. He rested there for a moment, watching and listening, and when he was convinced that he had disturbed no one, he was up and moving again.

In seconds he was at the base of the berm. On the other side of it was the SA-2. Fetterman could see the nose of the missile and the four miniature stabilizing fins on the nose cone. Patiently he waited in case someone, a guard, a technician, a soldier out for a smoke, had seen him working his way to the berm, but no one appeared to search for him. No alarms went off and no searchlights blazed. The site remained dark and quiet.

Slowly, his rifle held in his hands, he used his elbows and feet to crawl up the berm. He froze at the top, expecting to find barbed wire or booby traps, but apparently the North Vietnamese didn't fear saboteurs or guerrilla attacks.

He slid down the berm and found himself sitting on the ground no more than six or eight feet from the side of the missile. It was about thirty-five feet long and slightly over two feet in diameter. It was painted gray with a mottling of green and black to camouflage it from the air. The erector was dark green and looked flimsy. Fetterman moved to it and touched it, expecting to feel cool metal, but instead found rough plywood. For a moment he was confused and then looked again at the missile. It was a fake.

"Son of a bitch," he whispered. He had penetrated a dummy missile site. He slipped forward so that he was in the shadows thrown by the missile. The berm formed a semicircle with a paved road leading into the open end. That was for the trucks that brought the replacement missiles. To one side was a bunker of some kind. Constructed of concrete, it didn't look as if it belonged on the dummy site. Fetterman worked his way toward it.

On the side closest to the road was a metal door with a long metal bar across it. Fetterman lifted the bar and the door swung open with a whisper of well-oiled hinges. He entered the building but too little light filtered through the open door. There was a glint of light off metal and the smell of oil and dust. He couldn't see what was stored in the building. He knew that it wasn't a real SA-2 because the structure was too short for that. When he reached out, he touched a cool metal tube that was pointed at one end. He ran a hand along it and found short triangles of metal at the other end.

Using the available light, he bent close and tried to see what he had found. Compared to the mock-up outside, this was a miniature missile not more than five feet long. The diameter and configuration seemed to indicate an SA-7.

More confused now, Fetterman backed out the door and closed it. He crouched at the side of the building, listening to the sounds around him. By craning, he could see down the road to another of the missile launch areas. The whole SA-2 site would have six missiles and a command center. The thing to do was find the command center and see if it was an active one or another mock-up.

USING THE AVAILABLE COVER and crawling rather than walking, it took Gerber's team nearly an hour to cross the short distance from their hiding place to the berm guarding the missile. When they reached it, Gerber sent Tyme around the outside one way and Krung around the other. After they both disappeared into the darkness, Gerber, Bocker and Kit began a slow, quiet climb up the hard-packed earth.

When they reached the top, they slipped over and scrambled down the side. While Kit covered them, Gerber and Bocker scrambled to the side of the missile. Bocker put a foot up on the erector, heard the wooden thud and dropped back to the ground.

"Something's wrong here, Captain," he whispered.

Gerber moved forward and touched the plywood and then reached up to pat the side of the missile.

"Dummies."

"Sir?"

"Those CIA and Air Force dummies gave us the location of a dummy site."

At that moment both Krung and Tyme appeared. They took up positions at the opening in the berm to cover the team inside. Bocker watched them and then put his lips only an inch from Gerber's ear, "Now what?"

Gerber sat with his back against the plywood and looked at his watch. Twelve minutes after one. There was no way they could get to one of the other sites that the CIA had wanted them to explore. Moving at night with the caution that would be necessary, would take them three or four days to travel the seventy miles to the secondary target.

"Captain?" asked Bocker.

Gerber wanted to shout at him, to tell him to shut up and let him think, but knew it would do no good. Bocker wanted instructions and Gerber didn't have any. He took a deep breath of the night air that now held the hint of a chill.

"Let's explore the whole site. Maybe they erected a couple of dummy launchers to fool the Weasels. Maybe the real missile launchers are somewhere else."

With Kit and Bocker trailing behind him, Gerber moved to the entrance. He fell into a position next to Tyme as the young sergeant watched for the enemy.

Gerber examined the whole site. To his left the rise of a berm ring protected another missile. There wasn't much of anything to the right. An open field that had been planted with crops. In the center of it was a clump of trees and bushes that could conceal the headquarters and workshops, if this was more than just a dummy site.

From the left came a quiet voice. "Captain, I have good news and I have bad news."

Startled, Gerber rolled away, landing hard on his left elbow as he swung his weapon up. Fetterman materialized out of the gloom and shadows at the side of the berm.

"Christ, Tony," whispered Gerber, "I could have filled you full of holes."

"Had faith in you, Captain," said Fetterman, grinning. "You didn't shoot in North Carolina when I surprised you there, so I figured you wouldn't shoot here."

"So what's your news?"

"This is a dummy site. No real SA-2s on it at all. That's the bad news."

"You check the command vehicles and the maintenance sheds?" asked Gerber.

"Haven't gotten there yet, but I doubt they'll be manned," said Fetterman. He stopped talking and looked toward the center of the site. "You know, Captain, I found a bunch of SA-7s stored near one of those plywood Guidelines. That's the good news. I found real missiles here."

"So?" Then it dawned on Gerber. "The SA-7 is a shoulder-fired weapon. There has got to be someone around here to shoot it."

"Exactly."

He thought about that. No SA-2s, only the plywood mock-ups, but real SA-7s. Something about that troubled him. It made Gerber feel he had the answers he had been sent to find.

However, this wasn't the time to dwell on it. He had other things to worry about. He stared at Fetterman. "You find a sign of either Duc or Barlett?"

"No, sir. Ran into an NVA officer who had found Barlett's knife..."

"His knife?"

"I saw him pick it up. It looked like it was Barlett's knife. I thought Barlett might have dropped it while he was in the air. There was no sign of his body anywhere, or that of Duc. I had to kill the officer. I didn't want him running around with that knife."

Gerber shook his head, thinking about what Fetterman had just told him. The missing men were still missing. The only sign of them was the knife that Fetterman said the NVA officer had had. That bothered him greatly.

"That officer was alone?" asked Gerber.

"There was someone with him in the forest that I never saw, but no one came looking for him."

"I don't like it."

"Sorry, Captain, but there was nothing I could do. He had Barlett's knife and was coming right at me. I figured that if he disappeared, it would be more confusing if he disappeared completely for a couple of days."

There was more that Gerber wanted to know, but it wasn't the time or place for it.

"Okay, Tony, take the point. Justin, you've got the rear again. Bocker, Kit and I will follow in the center. Tony, you spot anyone, either take him out or take cover and we'll rethink this thing."

Fetterman glided to the right past Gerber and the opening in the berm. There was another of the concrete sheds that Fetterman was sure contained more of the SA-7s. He passed it and drifted along the edge of the road, a light gray ribbon that twisted and turned, and then stopped. He heard a bubble of laughter and then loud chattering in Vietnamese. Through a gap in the vegetation, he saw a single dim light bobbing like a lantern being carried by someone.

A moment later Gerber joined him and together they examined the tiny camp. There were several trucks, Soviet ZIL-151s that resembled a deuce and a half. They were covered with canvas covers and had wooden steps leading up into them. It looked as if they had been there for quite a while. Grass and weeds grew around the tires, which were low. The vegetation at the foot of the steps was worn away from frequent use. Apparently sometimes the rear of the ZILs were used as maintenance workshops and repair sheds for the SAM sites.

Beyond them were several squad tents. They were canvas and surrounded by wooden walkways. From the interior of one came a diffused glow. Low voices, men talking quietly came from there. Not far from the tents were the Fan Song and Spoon Rest radars and their control vans. It seemed ridiculous to have those radars on a site that was little more than a fake.

Fetterman pointed to them and asked, "Are those dummies, too?"

"Hidden in the trees? I don't think so. This whole thing makes very little sense."

"What'll we do?"

"Infiltrate," said Gerber. "Slowly and quietly. Take out anyone who is moving around and then use grenades on the tent if anyone spots us. We kill everyone and then examine this site carefully."

"Wouldn't it make more sense to fall back? There's nothing here for us."

"Tony, I don't like this setup. A dummy site would have all fake missiles. There wouldn't be any real ones on it. It would have the berm and the roadwork because each of those can be seen from the air or in photos. Without them, the site is flawed and our Intel people could tell in a minute. But the radar vans are usually hidden. A fake site doesn't need them because they wouldn't be readily visible. I want to find out why they're here."

"Shouldn't we just pull out and let the spooks figure out what is going on?"

"They're going to ask us some very difficult questions. Since we're here already, let's see if we can find some answers. Then we get out." But even as he said it, he realized that he had all the information that anyone could want. The answer was buried in there somewhere.

"Yes, sir."

Bocker joined them then. He glanced at both of them but didn't say a word.

"Galvin, once we've got the site secured, I want you to examine those radar vans. Make sure that the proper electronic gear is in them."

"Yes, sir."

Gerber eased back then, his eyes on the campsite. He located the rest of the team and explained the plan. He told each of them that they would attack quietly from all sides, using their knives. At the first sound of firing, they would each attack the squad tents with automatic weapons and grenades. If no one fired, they would discover what they could and then slip into the night so that the Vietnamese wouldn't know they had been around.

When each member of the team understood the instructions, Gerber told them to fan out and begin the recon of the site. Without another word each member of the group faded into the dark. Gerber watched them and then began to crawl to the trucks parked close to him. As he reached them he listened, but could hear no evidence of anyone working inside. He then crawled under one of them, working his way to the front where he could see the squad tent. He looked at his watch and realized that the assault would begin in less than a minute.

10

SA-2 GUIDELINE MISSILE
COMPLEX NEAR KE SAT
NORTH VIETNAM

Bocker killed the sentry.

It was a simple thing to do. He waited until the soldier passed him, then he rose quietly, grabbing the man from behind. With his hand over the enemy's mouth and nose, Bocker jerked him backward as he levered his knee into the small of the man's back. As he collapsed onto the fulcrum of Bocker's knee, Bocker cut his throat. There was the whisper of ripped silk as the knife slashed the delicate flesh. The man spasmed as his hot blood washed over Bocker's hand and down his chest.

It took the man a moment to die. He jerked right and left and heaved himself upward, trying to escape from Bocker's grip. Then he stopped struggling and was still. There was no tickle on Bocker's hand as the man tried to breathe. Just a rattle deep in his throat as the lungs collapsed and the heart stopped beating.

Bocker dragged him into the deep grass at the edge of the camp and stripped him of his weapon and knife. Not wanting to be burdened by the extra weight of the dead man's AK, Bocker broke it open and slipped the trigger housing and receiver group from the weapon, dropping the pieces into the grass and mud to hide them.

He moved forward again to the side of the van where the operator of the Fan Song radar would work. He pressed an ear against the thin metal but heard nothing inside. Satisfied that the van was empty, he skirted it and moved closer to the tent. When he was ten or twelve feet away he dropped to the grass and waited. From the inside, he could hear a little noise and the uneven, discordant strains of Vietnamese music. The movement of the men inside threw an ever-changing pattern of shadows on the canvas of the tents.

GERBER PULLED HIMSELF from under the truck and worked his way to the left, along the line of vehicles. He stopped near the last one and watched as one of his people came around the corner of the generator shed. It was a structure with a thatched roof and support poles around its perimeter. The sides were open, giving a full view of the generator that sat inside. It was not running.

The team member, crouched in the darkness at the edge of the shed and waited. Gerber was sure that it was Krung. A solitary enemy soldier approached from the other direction, a red glow between his fingers. When the enemy soldier stopped walking and leaned against the pole of the shed, Gerber's man struck.

There was a flash of movement and then a muffled choke, almost a cough, escaped from the guard who dropped his cigarette. He slid down the pole and Gerber's soldier lost his grip on the enemy. He rolled to the right, his foot drumming on the hard wood of the support. To Gerber it sounded as if he was banging on a bass drum, the sound echoing through the night, but there was no reaction from the men in the tent.

A moment later the team member emerged from the shadows and dropped into the grass, almost disappearing. Gerber followed the movement until his soldier halted a few feet from the squad tent.

The enemy soldier's body was in plain sight at the edge of the generator shed, but there wasn't anyone around to see it. Gerber crept forward then, moving on his belly and keeping his eyes moving. He slipped toward the shed and when he was close, caught the odor of fresh blood. He dragged the corpse into the shadows where it would be found less easily.

He stopped and surveyed the area. A faked missile site with men and radar all over it. Fetterman had found missiles of a different variety. There were questions that had to be answered, but Gerber didn't think he'd find them on the site. The best course of action now was pull everyone back and get the hell out. He figured he already had the answers and didn't know it.

He crawled back to the shed until he was close to the tent, nearly in front of the open flap that served as a door. Here he halted and rolled to his right. At that moment a man wearing a dark undershirt appeared in front of the tent. He held a cigarette between his lips. Fiddling with his fly he turned and began to urinate into the grass at the side of the boardwalk. At the sound of a shout from inside the tent, he looked over his shoulder.

Hastily he buttoned his fly and pulled the cigarette from his mouth. Suddenly he froze, staring into the dark. He took a step forward, off the boardwalk and then spun, leaping for the tent, shouting at the men inside.

Gerber jerked a grenade from his belt, pulled the pin and dropped it. His eyes on the tent, he let the spoon fly, mentally counted to two and tossed the grenade through the flap of the tent.

As it bounced on the wooden planking, there was a single shout of fear. Gerber dropped his face to the ground and the weapon detonated. He heard the shrapnel rip through the sides of the tent, men crying out in pain. Cries of anguish pierced the air as a second and third grenade went off, thrown by others on Gerber's team.

Gerber was on his feet, retreating. He dived for cover near the trucks, his weapon up and ready. A flicker of movement to the right caught his eye. Krung appeared, running across the open ground. He threw himself to the earth and opened fire with his AK, raking the sides of the tent that was beginning to burn.

Now Gerber realized that it was Kit who had killed the guard. It explained why the death of the enemy had been a little sloppy. Krung would have made a clean job of it.

Two men dived from the tent, rolling into the grass. There was a burst of fire and the copper-jacketed rounds slammed into the trucks behind him. Gerber ducked and came up firing. As he ducked, the enemy turned on him. He pushed his face into the soft, moist earth.

From the right there was a second burst from an AK. The ground around the enemy soldiers exploded. They returned the fire, the muzzle flashes lighting them like a strobe.

Gerber was up on his knees, his finger on the trigger. He held it down, aiming at the two NVA soldiers. He saw one of them hit. He flipped to his side, his weapon flying from his fingers.

The other man spun, aiming at Gerber, but caught a burst in the side of the head. He shrieked and dropped into the grass.

There was a wild burst from the rear of the tent, answered by the hammering of more AKs. Green tracers ripped into it. The shooting increased until the night was filled with the sound of it, and then suddenly, it all stopped.

For a moment it was quiet around him, the only sound was the building roar of the fire as it gained momentum, consuming the tent. A lone figure rushed out of the tent, screaming, his body ablaze. He fell from the boardwalk, rolled over, setting some of the grass on fire. The stench of roasting flesh drifted over to Gerber.

A figure came running from the far end of the complex, his weapon held high. He slowed, then headed straight for the burning tent, yelling at the top of his voice. Krung stood in front of him and shouted in Vietnamese. At close range he cut the soldier down, the flame from the barrel of his rifle stabbing out and brushing the enemy's shirt.

Gerber exploded into motion. He skirted the burning tent and ran toward the radar van. Bocker was standing at the foot of the wooden steps that led up into it, staring at the door.

"Anyone inside?" asked Gerber.

"I don't think so."

"Then go."

Bocker leaped up the steps, grabbed the knob and ripped open the door. Gerber followed him and dived through. He moved to the right and collided with a rack of equipment. A metal object dropped to the floor and rolled away with a clatter, but even in the darkness, Gerber could tell he was alone inside.

Bocker closed the door. A moment later there was a pencil-thin beam of light from Bocker's hand. He played it over the equipment, the radio gear and the radar screens and said, "Looks like the real thing. This hasn't been faked."

Gerber climbed to his feet. "Yeah. This is a real van but equipped with dummy missiles."

"And a concrete building with SA-7s," said Bocker. He was on his knees, checking the wiring to make sure it was all there, although he couldn't see any purpose in mocking up the equipment in the van since it couldn't be seen from the air.

"Let's get out of here," said Gerber. "We'll collect our people and get off the site."

The ex-filtration was simple. Gerber's group watched the burned tent collapse and the flames die. There were no further threats from the NVA soldiers. Convinced that the enemy were either dead or had fled, Gerber ordered his men to retreat.

From the command center of the missile complex, they entered the tall grass that bordered a farmer's field, diverted to the left and worked their way between the rows of the knee-high crops. At the tree line, they spread out, waiting for signs of pursuit. But nothing happened. The fire from the tent then spread to the truck park and generator shed and those burned quickly and brightly for a few minutes. Then the glow faded as those flames died, too.

Gerber felt an overwhelming need to get away from the missile site. He told Tyme to take the point and they started toward the east rapidly, using the fading moonlight and starlight to navigate. As the sky paled, Tyme found them a hiding place for the day. It was a thick copse of trees and bushes in the middle of the forest. A clear stream bubbled close to them. Gerber nodded his approval and they moved in, fanning into a loose circle with half the team on alert while the other half ate and then slept.

Bocker crawled to Gerber and whispered to him, "We can make the six o'clock check-in, Captain."

"What do you need to do?"

"Run the wire antenna up a tree and weave it among the branches. Won't be visible from the ground."

"Would anyone be able to get a fix on us because of it?"

"No, sir. We'll only be receiving and not transmitting. If we transmit and someone happens to be set on the frequency, they could triangulate, if they were prepared to do it. If we stayed on the air long enough."

Gerber took a deep breath and exhaled slowly. His muscles ached from the activity of last night. His eyes felt like someone had poured sand into them. The sweat he had worked up during the fight had dried, leaving a sticky, itchy film over his body. At times he could smell his own body odor. His black uniform was stained with mud, kerosene and ripped in two or three places. The very last thing he wanted to do was climb a tree with Bocker's wire antenna.

"You get it up," said Gerber.

Bocker grinned as if he had just been given a three-day pass. "I'll let you know when we're ready."

He turned and scrambled off until he reached a large tree with clumps of pine needles that looked like leaves from a distance. Since the branches hung close to the ground, Bocker could easily hoist himself up into it. He climbed high quickly disappearing from sight. A moment later he reappeared, dropped to the earth and worked his way back to Gerber, detouring long enough to pick up some of his equipment.

When he reached Gerber, he sat and plugged the leads from the wire antenna into the radio. He handed an earpiece and a splitter to Gerber, then, plugging another earpiece into the splitter, he plugged it all into the jack on the radio. He turned it on, adjusted the volume so that there was a quiet buzz from the static as he played with the gain knob and then only the hiss of the carrier wave.

For a while there was absolutely nothing to be heard. Then, quietly, sounding more like an insect buzzing from long distance, they heard their call sign.

"Diablo, Diablo, this is Cheyenne. Stand by for a message in three parts. Diablo, this is Cheyenne. Stand by for a message in three parts. Break. Break."

Gerber put a hand to his ear, pushing the tiny earphone in deeper and holding it there so that he could hear better. He cocked his head to one side and closed his eyes in order to concentrate.

"Part one," said the radio operator. "Aircrews downed in your vicinity. If possible locate as many as feasible and escort out. From original target, bearing one-two-five and one-seven-zero, twenty to twenty-five klicks."

Bocker shot a glance at Gerber, who nodded. He had understood the message. The paper pushers in Saigon wanted him to try to find downed aircrews and escort them all out of North Vietnam.

"Part two. Target changed to Lima Lima five-eight six-one. I say again, target changed to Lima Lima five-eight six-one."

That figured, thought Gerber. Send us on one mission and then have us check out something else. With the edge of his hand, he scraped some of the dried grass away so that he could write the numbers in the dirt.

"Part three. Royal Palace asks you to investigate the detention of our nationals at Saigon Sheraton. Code name Involved. Message ends."

Gerber pulled the map from his pocket and checked the grid references. They had designed their own grid system so that anyone listening in wouldn't be able to plot anything unless they happened to have a map with a similar grid. And only Maxwell and Gerber had them.

He ran a finger down the map and located the new target. It was near Hoa Binh, sixty or seventy miles to the west. Someone in Saigon wasn't looking at the map. There was no way that Gerber could travel south and southeast on one mission, then turn west for a second and back to the north for a third. It would require traveling over a hundred miles in enemy territory while more of the North Vietnamese army joined in the search.

Bocker switched off the radio and asked, "What was that Saigon Sheraton nonsense?"

Gerber couldn't help grinning. "An oblique reference to the Hanoi Hilton, I believe. I think they would like us to try to spring some of our people from it."

"My God," said Bocker, his face suddenly pale. "They want us to infiltrate Hanoi, find the POW compound and try to free the men, and still want us to hike to the coast?"

"If it's not too much trouble."

"What are we going to do?" asked Bocker.

Gerber didn't have a quick answer for that. He was in place and had the chance to do it. But he didn't have the information. No one had briefed him or his team on the Hanoi Hilton. All he knew was that it was on the southeast side of Hanoi, but he didn't know where for sure. He didn't know how many guards there were, what the routine was, or even where inside the Americans were being held. It was a pipe dream thought up by someone sitting in an airconditioned office in Saigon. Someone who had a bright idea and had the power to see that it was sent down the chain of command.

But there was nothing that Gerber could do, no matter how much he'd like to help the prisoners. If he tried, the best he could hope for would be some of his team surviving to be taken prisoner. At worst, they would all die in the attempt. Nothing would be gained by it. He rejected the idea.

"We'll rest here for the remainder of the day and then head out tonight," he said. "We'll try to find those downed crewmen, but I can't see us trying to get to the other missile site or trying to break into the Hanoi Hilton. It won't work."

"What are you going to tell them in Saigon?"

"That we had to get our butts out of North Vietnam before we joined those men in Hanoi. Besides, we've got some good information for the Intel boys."

THE KNOCKING AT HER DOOR forced Robin awake. She rolled to her side, opened her eyes and stared across the room, but didn't get up. Instead she shoved her hands between her thighs and tried to go back to sleep, but the hammering continued until she shouted, "All right."

She climbed out of bed and slipped on the jungle fatigue jacket she used for a robe. Since it was large, it hung to mid-thigh. Fumbling with the buttons, she stumbled to the door. Before opening it, she ran a hand through her hair, trying to straighten it slightly.

Robin opened the door to find George standing there, his hand poised to knock again. She left the door open and walked back to the bed, her head pounding. She sat on the bed, yawning. When George was inside, she asked, "What in hell are you doing here so early?"

"We've got a noon deadline on the story and we need to find out a few things." He looked at her, staring at her ankles, and then slowly moving his eyes upward until they were on her face. "Christ, you're good looking," he said, the awe obvious in his voice. "I woke you up?"

"What d'you want, a testimonial? Yes, you woke me up."

"You look about ten times better than any woman I've ever seen when she's just gotten up. You looking for a husband or live-in lover?"

"George," she said tiredly, "You've got a wife waiting for you in the States." She smiled. "And for all I know, you've got one waiting for you here, too."

"Not here," said George. "You got any coffee?"

She pointed to the tiny kitchen off the main room. George looked at the heavily lacquered cabinets, searched through a couple of them, and found little except canned fruit and juice. Finally, he saw a tin of coffee. He ran water in the chipped sink and then filled the pot. He added the coffee and plugged it in. That finished, he walked back into the combination bedroom-sitting room and dropped into the only chair that wasn't covered with books, magazines or clothes. He glimpsed a pair of mesh bikini panties that would hardly conceal anything and wished that he could see Robin modeling them.

For a moment she studied George and then stood up. She located a pair of khaki pants and slipped them on without giving George anything to look at. She turned her back to him and let the fatigue jacket fall to the floor so that he could see her bare back.

"Jesus, what in the hell happened to you?"

Too late, she remembered the network of puckered scars that marked her back, hips and backside. Because she couldn't see them, she often forgot they were there. As she pulled on a white blouse, she said, "Something that happened a couple of years ago. No big deal."

"No big deal," said George. "It looks like you were—"

"It's something I'd prefer not to talk about." She spun on him, buttoning her blouse. "Okay?"

"Sure. Fine." He got to his feet. "I'll look at the coffee."

"What's your plan for today?"

His voice, muffled because he was in the other room, was still strong. "Thought it would be nice to talk to the B-Team commander here and see what he has to say. Talk to the folks over at MACV-SOG and quiz them. Let some things drop and maybe we'll have scared them enough to tell us some more.''

He reappeared carrying two cups of coffee. He held one out to Robin. ''Here's your eye-opener.''

George sat down again and took a long sip from his coffee. He let his eyes roam over the clutter in the room. There was a table littered with books and papers. A portable typewriter sat in front of the chair. Beer cans and empty whiskey bottles were lined up against one wall. The shutters were closed and the air conditioner was on, but did little to dissipate the heat of the room. George was sweating heavily now, but Robin didn't seem to notice the heat.

He suddenly felt bothered by this woman. The scars on her back had done it. She'd seen more of this war than he had. He hoped that he'd never see it as closely as she had. Now he was afraid that she was a woman on the verge of a collapse. The way she lived, the haphazard way she pursued her career, the scars, all suggested something was going on below the surface. From the evidence, it was obvious that the captain she was chasing had something to do with it. George wondered if the captain suspected Robin Morrow's mental condition.

As the silence between them broadened and then became uncomfortable, Robin set her coffee cup on the floor and disappeared into the bathroom. She didn't say a word to George. He sat quietly waiting for her, wondering if he should derail the investigation now that he understood some of her motives.

Robin returned a few minutes later looking even better than before. She grinned at George, showing him her perfect white teeth and said, ''Ready to go?''

George gulped the last of his coffee and said, ''If you are, then I am.''

WHILE GERBER AND FETTERMAN discussed the new orders, which they decided were stupid, Bocker was working with the radio, changing the frequencies and listening to the emergency channels, and trying to locate the downed crewmen. He knew that anyone down in North Vietnam would be broadcasting on 242.0, letting everyone know they needed help. If he could pick up the signal, it would make the task of locating downed crews easier.

He had left his wire antenna in place. If worse came to worst, he could leave it there forever and let the North Vietnamese wonder about it if they ever found it. The only thing wrong with it was that he couldn't turn it for a directional bearing on the signal, if he found one. He would have to make voice contact and get directions then, if possible.

With the earpiece in place and the radio set, there was nothing more that he could do. He sat with his back against the trunk of a rough-barked tree and ate some of his C-rations. As he spooned the bland-tasting boned chicken from the can, he listened to the carrier wave telling him that they were receiving, if anyone ever bothered to transmit a call for help.

Of course, the downed crewmen had the same problem that Bocker had. To transmit invited eavesdropping. A clever North Vietnamese, with a radio and a directional antenna, could do a lot for the men searching in the field. Two NVAs narrowed the search zone and a third would be able to pinpoint the transmitter.

But, if the downed men wanted to escape from North Vietnam, they had to transmit. If the air rescue people were running the show properly, the downed men would have been given a time to make contact with the SAR forces. They would make one or two quick calls and then the rescue choppers and the covering fighters would come in.

Finally he heard a two-tone wailing sound. A voice broke in requesting, "Beeper come up voice."

"This is Baron One."

"Say authentication number."

"Zero-six-one-two."

"Roger, Baron One. What was the first car you owned?"

"Ah, Mustang."

There was a pause, then the voice came back. "Say favorite football team."

"Broncos."

"Roger, Baron One. We have choppers inbound. Please come up again in one-five minutes. Do you copy?"

"Roger."

Bocker waited in silence, the white plastic spoon stuck in the forgotten can of boned chicken he held. The whole routine that he had listened to was the Air Force authentication system. Each pilot, crew chief, load master, everyone who was on flight status, had a card filed with all kinds of personal information on it. That card, and that information, was a classified document that would be given to the commander of the SAR forces before rescue. It was a way of ensuring that the man on the ground was not a decoy trying to suck in aircraft for an ambush. If the answers did not match, the SAR forces would refuse to land.

When nothing more was broadcast right away, Bocker shut off the radio to conserve the batteries and then worked his way to where Gerber and Fetterman sat, their heads together as they studied the map.

"Call sign of downed crew is Baron One," whispered Bocker. "Air rescue is trying to get in to him."

"You have any idea where he is?"

"Only that he's fairly close, based solely on the strength of the signal. But hell, sir, that could be caused by skip and he could be down around the DMZ."

"Any other information available? Anything at all?"

"No, sir. Air rescue advised him to come up again about ten minutes from now. I'll see what I can get."

"You going to try to contact him?" asked Fetterman.

"I don't think we should. But I'll keep monitoring."

"Okay," said Gerber. "And keep me advised. You get something a little more definite, let me know."

"Yes, sir."

"Tony, let's grab some sleep. We'll get started again about dusk. Galvin, you'll have to monitor the radio this afternoon, but you can trade with Justin later. I want everyone to catch a little sleep."

"Yes, sir."

Gerber watched the communications sergeant retreat into his hiding place. When he was gone, Gerber said, "I'm going to sleep first shift. You take second?"

"No problem, sir."

"The moment you get tired, wake me up. I've probably had more sleep lately than you."

Fetterman grinned. "That's only because you officers are by nature lazy."

Gerber crawled toward a bush and slithered under it. He rolled onto his back and felt the rough ground, broken twigs and dropped thorns pricking his skin. He rocked right and left, crushing them, and then closed his eyes. Although the sun was hidden by the bushes and the trees, he could feel the heat radiating through the leaves. Sweat broke out now that the early morning chill had burned off, and Gerber knew it was going to be a long, hot day. There was almost no breeze and what there was didn't reach him in the bush.

Before he closed his eyes, Kit slipped in beside him. She laid her head on his belly, her eyes open so that she was looking up at him. Gerber wanted her to find another hiding place, but didn't want the confrontation that was sure to follow. Instead he winked at her, telling her to stay, and then closed his eyes.

As he did, the images from the firefight the night before flashed in front of him. Not much of a fight. They had ambushed the enemy almost as they slept, killing them before they could respond. Not exactly the fairest way to fight a war, but one that the NVA and VC had used many times. Sneak up on a unit and cut the throats of the sleeping men. In fact, some of the more clever VC cut every other throat. It inspired terror in those left alive, and they communicated that terror to everyone they talked to.

He reminded himself that they were fighting a war and that was what happened in war. He forced the thoughts from his mind and briefly wondered about the new orders. There was no way he could carry out all three parts. Given the option, the part with the greatest likelihood of succeeding was to locate the downed crewmen and help them out. Exploring another missile complex or trying to break into the Hanoi Hilton wouldn't work.

As he thought about the dummy complex, he realized there was something that he had seen, or been told about, that should have bothered him. Something about it was wrong, but he didn't know what it was and before he could figure it out, he fell asleep.

11

Robin sat quietly while George Krupp did all the talking. She had no desire to flirt with Major Richard Palmer. Instead she studied his Spartan office. By MACV standards, it was a cubbyhole, furnished with a battered desk, two old chairs and a bookcase crammed with Army manuals. The walls were bare except for a single picture of John F. Kennedy. The lone window overlooked the parking lot and although the blinds were down, they weren't closed, so that the bright morning sun invaded the room.

"This afternoon," Krupp was saying, "we're putting a story on the courier plane that shows a group of our soldiers are operating illegally inside North Vietnam. Unless, of course, you can show me that my statement is wrong."

Palmer leaned back in his chair and laced his fingers behind his head. "Mr. Krupp, I have no knowledge of any of our teams currently operating north of the DMZ."

Krupp grinned. "A very precise answer."

"And a truthful one." Palmer dropped his feet to the dirty, tiled floor and leaned his elbows on his desk. "Look, we have people running around all over South Vietnam. We're engaged in trail-watching activities, and some of our men have gone into both Cambodia and Laos for that purpose. We've made no real secret of that. However, current regulations prohibit our men from operating in Cambodia, Laos and most especially, North Vietnam.''

"Then you're denying the report that a Special Forces team is in North Vietnam."

"I don't know how to make it any clearer to you." A smile creased Palmer's face. "Anything else?"

Krupp rubbed his chin and then flipped through his notebook. He glanced at Robin, then looked at the major again. "Yesterday morning a highly placed source suggested that a mission had been mounted into the North."

"Yes, I'm very familiar with your—meaning the press's—highly placed source. The catchall leak peddler who is never identified, or who can be blamed if the information turns out to be faulty."

Krupp jotted down what Palmer said and then stood. "Our story is going out today. Special Forces soldiers are working in North Vietnam. Anything you say, or anyone says, is going to sound like you're trying to cover up illegal operations on foreign soil."

The smile left Palmer's face. "That's irresponsible journalism. You'll be feeding the fires of discontent that already threaten to cripple our effort."

"Maybe the effort should be crippled," Krupp shot back.

"That's not for you to decide." Palmer slapped a hand to the desktop. "Who in the hell died and left you in charge? When did the press get the mandate to tell all, regardless of who suffered?"

"The people have the right to know."

"That's an old one," said Palmer. "The people's right to know stops where it conflicts with national security or my right to life."

"That, too, is an old one and you argue from your own self-interest on this. You want to make a statement, fine. If not, then the story goes out this afternoon."

Palmer looked at Morrow, who had spent the whole interview staring at the floor. Although he was addressing Krupp, he spoke to Morrow. "Can I say something off the record?"

"I don't like to start an interview and then go off the record," said George.

"And I don't like irresponsible reporters," snapped Palmer. "I'm not going to say anything you'll want to print."

"Then let's stay on the record."

"Fine. Miss Morrow?" When Robin looked up, Palmer said, "Miss Morrow, I know that you have a relationship with one of our officers, so I'm counting on you." He turned to stare at Krupp. "Mr. Krupp, as I said, I have no knowledge of any operations in North Vietnam run by the Special Forces, but that doesn't mean there isn't something going on."

Krupp was about to speak, but Palmer held up a hand to stop him. "No, what I'm trying to say is that by printing your story in the blind, so to speak, you might be compromising security. It's the reason that we tell our men who are captured not to make up lies for the enemy. First, a skilled interrogator will eventually penetrate the lies. And second, by making up something that sounds convincing, you might inadvertently compromise some other mission."

Krupp shook his head. "What a load of shit."

"Believe what you want," said Palmer. "But I do know that we have pilots on the ground in North Vietnam right now, fighting for their lives, and if you print your story, you're going to make it that much harder to get them out."

Krupp was going to protest again and then realized that Palmer had let something slip. "Pilots on the ground. You have names and units?"

"I have nothing. It's an Air Force matter. But right now, those men are trying to evade the NVA. A story in the American press, broadcast all over the world, is going to be heard in Hanoi, and even if your facts about a covert mission are wrong, you're going to damage our chances of getting those men out safely."

"How long?" asked Krupp.

"How long what?"

"How long do I have to sit on this? I put it on the courier plane at noon, it'll be on the morning news tomorrow. I delay until a later flight, maybe the news tomorrow night."

"I could call you when it's safe."

"Not good enough, Major. Then others will have the story, too."

"Then check with me this afternoon. But please don't write your story yet."

George Krupp got to his feet again. "I'll call you this afternoon. Please don't try to avoid me or my call or I write my story. And I'll be expecting a better answer from you about this."

Palmer stood up and extended his hand across the desk. "Thank you for understanding. I'll try to find something to make it worth your while." He glanced at Robin who was now standing, too. "Nice to meet you, Miss Morrow. Hope to see you again soon."

FETTERMAN STOPPED AT THE EDGE of the bush and spoke in a stage whisper. "Somebody's coming."

Gerber was awake in an instant, his hand reaching for the AK near him. He felt the pressure of Kit's head on his belly, but hadn't moved enough to awaken her.

"How many and how far?" he asked quietly.

"At least a dozen at two hundred yards, maybe a little less."

Gerber reached down and touched Kit's shoulder, knowing as he did that she was now awake, too. She rolled away from him and froze facedown, her palms pressed to the ground in case she needed to move quickly.

"What kind of formation?"

"Looks like some type of search party, Captain, but I don't think they expect to find anything. They seem to be going through the motions, and aren't paying much attention to that, either."

"What do you think is our best course of action?" Gerber trusted Fetterman's judgment.

"I think we should spread out a little more and let them walk past us. They're not exactly beating the bushes. If we're quiet, I think they'll miss us."

"Kit, you stay here. Crawl in as deep as you can and don't move. Shoot if you have to, but try to avoid it. We don't want to get into a firefight now."

She nodded her understanding and then shifted around so that she was next to the base of the bush. She snagged her weapon and pulled it around, the barrel pointing out. Gerber slipped forward into the open. He had expected the air to change, but it was no cooler or warmer in the open than it had been under the bush. There was no breeze blowing. Only the humidity settling on him like a warm, wet blanket.

"Where's Bocker?"

Fetterman smiled and pointed. "Climbed the tree with his antenna, reeling it in as he went up. Totally invisible from the ground."

"Tyme?"

"Took Krung and moved to the west to the other side of the stream. There's good cover for them there."

Gerber looked to the west but couldn't see a thing. He didn't like the way the team was spread out. That would make it hard for them to support one another if a fight developed, but then, if one or two were caught, the others might get away. He sacrificed unit integrity for the possibility of escape.

"Okay, Tony," he said. "Let's you and me head to the south and east."

Fetterman nodded and took off quickly. Gerber turned to make a rapid survey of where they had been. Nothing was lying around to give them away. Nothing pointed to the bush where Kit hid, and there were no footprints leading to the stream. Satisfied they had cleaned up after themselves, Gerber followed the master sergeant, dodging among the trees and bushes as they fled deeper into the forest.

Up ahead, there was a slight depression in the ground with a bush and a rock at one end. Fetterman pointed to it and grinned, disappearing into it before Gerber could react. As Gerber went by, he could see no sign of Fetterman. In fact, he knew that Fetterman could extract himself from the hiding place quietly if he had to.

A moment later Gerber found a hiding place for himself. An outcropping of tented rocks with several large bushes that provided good cover. If he was rushed from the front, he could escape through the rear while the stones on the sides would protect him. He crawled in and waited patiently, quietly, for the enemy to appear, or for the sound of gunfire if they discovered part of his team.

Lying there, his face close to the dank earth, he felt his heart pounding. Sweat poured from his face and down his sides and he wanted a drink. He wanted to scream, to shoot, to do something rather than lie there quietly. He shifted around so that he could see into the forest.

It seemed to take them forever. Gerber's back began to itch like he was lying in a patch of nettle. His ears twitched at the sounds of the forest as the animals ran from the men or chased one another. He could hear the buzzing of flying insects and saw a single spider inch its way up the rough surface of the rocks.

Suddenly there was a burst of laughter and a shout in Vietnamese. From the sound of the voice, Gerber knew it wasn't a warning and from the new laughs, that it had to be some kind of joke. An instant later the first of the NVA soldiers appeared.

Unlike those who were assigned to units in the South, these soldiers wore badges of rank and unit identification. One man had bright yellow shoulder boards with a red border. From the single stripe and the two stars on it, Gerber knew that the man was a North Vietnamese first lieutenant. The officer also wore a pistol in a holster held up by a belt with a red star in the center of the buckle.

Next to him was a sergeant. He was a burly man, much older than his lieutenant, with a face that had been scarred badly. He had blue shoulder boards with three stripes on them. Like the lieutenant, he was wearing dark green fatigues with collar tabs.

The rest of the men were scattered too far and wide for Gerber to see much detail. One might have been a corporal from the way he talked and gestured to the others. Each of them carried an SKS carbine, except for the sergeant, who had a new looking AK-47.

The thing that surprised Gerber the most was their boots. He had expected Ho Chi Minh sandals, but instead they were wearing canvas shoes that looked like high-topped basketball shoes. Gerber suspected that the design was stolen from the French since the boots looked like the lightweight patrol shoe used by the Foreign Legion.

As they came closer to him, Gerber saw that the officer wore the collar insignia of the cavalry. Inside a red parallelogram were the crossed sabers and horseshoe that marked a NVA cavalry officer. Gerber wondered if the man was a horseman, if he could actually ride one, or if the North Vietnamese Army had changed the cavalry as much as the U.S. Army had.

One of the privates sat at the base of a tree, his back against the trunk. He lit a cigarette and took a few puffs. Suddenly the sergeant was next to him, almost nose to nose, shouting at him. The private looked startled, jumped to his feet and then handed the cigarette to the sergeant. The NCO took a deep drag, exhaled and handed it back to the private. Both men laughed and then rushed through the trees making enough noise to wake the dead.

If Fetterman's theory was right and these men were a search party, they would never find anything. They made too much noise and weren't looking very hard. When they finally disappeared and Gerber could hear them no longer, he crawled from his hiding place, picked up Fetterman and headed back to round up the rest of the team.

Once they were gathered together and hidden behind a screen of bushes covered with bright orange flowers, Gerber told them, "I think we'd better get out of here. We're still too close to the SAM site at Ke Sat and to the roads leading to it. Apparently no one has discovered the fight there yet because those guys weren't looking too hard." He hesitated, studying the faces of the people with him. They seemed to be waiting for him to give them their orders.

"Galvin, what's the status of the men on the ground?"

"Haven't been picked up yet, sir. Triple A and MiGs have kept our people from getting in. That is, up to forty minutes ago. At that time we were still in radio contact."

Gerber took out his map and studied it quickly. "Justin, I want you up on the point. Sergeant Krung right behind. Kit and I will make up the middle element with Sergeant Bocker and then Sergeant Fetterman in the rear. Compass course of one two five. Questions?"

"You sure we should be moving in the daylight?" asked Tyme.

"No, especially with search parties out. But it'll be dark in a couple of hours and I don't like the proximity of the SAM site. We're still too close to it. We'll risk moving in the daylight, staying to the cover and moving very carefully and quietly."

"Captain," said Fetterman, "we've got a fairly large, known enemy force nearby."

"I know that, Sergeant, but I don't want to risk a firefight with them. We let them roam unharmed and everyone feels safer. If they all suddenly disappear, or we get into a firefight with them, we'll have a division in here looking for us. Right now, it seems to be their second string searching for lost pilots and that's the way I'd like it to stay."

"Yes, sir. Thought I should mention it."

"And that's why you've got the rear guard action. Make sure those guys don't sneak up on us. Make sure they don't find our trail. If you have to, take them out, but I'd prefer that we didn't."

"Understood."

"If there is nothing else, Sergeant Tyme, please move out. Remember, slow, easy and quiet."

GEORGE KRUPP SAT ACROSS THE TABLE from Robin and studied her closely. She hadn't spoken much during the day, avoiding eye contact with him and avoiding attempts to draw her out. Now she picked at the food in front of her and sipped at the rapidly warming beer.

"Robin, what's gotten into you?"

She took a drink and set the glass on the table, watching the bubbles rise in the beer. Finally she looked at George and said, "I'm not convinced that we should be following this story so closely."

"Why not?"

"It's just as Major Palmer said. We might be endangering some men without realizing it."

"You mean your Captain Gerber and his boys?"

She smiled weakly. "Not necessarily. But that doesn't make any difference. Palmer was right. When did we become so knowledgeable that we could make life and death decisions for everyone?"

"When did the Army? Or the government?"

"At least the government has some legitimacy," she said. "It wasn't self-appointed."

Krupp put down his fork and looked at her. "I'm not going to do anything to intentionally hurt anyone, but I am going to get the story. If we don't keep the pressure on, then those elected officials are going to think they're above the law and we'll be no better off than the people in Russia."

"I'm only saying that we should go easy until we're sure that we're not accidentally hurting someone."

"What's really on your mind?" asked Krupp. "This isn't about some unidentified pilots who might have bailed out over North Vietnam."

Robin started to tell him. The words formed in her mind and she could hear herself speak them, but before they got to her mouth, they were gone. She couldn't tell George about her love for Gerber, or how her heart had soared when he reappeared in Vietnam. She couldn't tell him that she knew he was free of her sister because Gerber had left her in the States without even a farewell phone call. There were so many strange twists and turns to the relationship that she had no idea where it was going. All she knew was that if Gerber happened to be in North Vietnam and was killed there, she would not have the opportunity to explore those feelings with him.

Instead of all that, she said, "We shouldn't file our story until we're sure of the facts. Even if someone else beats us, we have to be sure of what we know."

"I can live with that, Robin."

She finished her beer. "Then let's go over to the embassy and see what they have to say. If we hurry, we can still make the evening press briefing."

TYME HEARD THE ENEMY SOLDIER, and dropped to the soft forest floor, the decaying vegetation cushioning him. He slipped to the right until his side was against a hardwood tree. A lacy fern, dripping moisture, was directly in front of him. He could smell the rotting vegetation, the damp dirt and wet bark on the tree.

As he inched toward the sound that he had heard, he was careful not to put all his weight down at once. He moved slowly, cautiously shifting his hands, hips, knees and feet until he was sure he would make no noise. To move silently in a jungle, or forest, required total concentration. It could take him an hour to move fifty feet, but he didn't have to crawl that far.

Then, in a clearing, he saw a single man dressed in a green fatigue uniform. He wouldn't have been concerned, except the man wore a chest pouch that held three AK-47 banana magazines, a rucksack, and an entrenching tool. The noise he had heard was the quiet tap of the tool against the rounded, metal canteen on his hip.

Tyme slipped away and eased to the left. Movement caught his eye and he spotted another NVA soldier. Tyme froze, one hand out in front of him as the enemy pushed aside the branches of a bush, his hands fumbling with the buckle of his belt. As Tyme looked up, his eyes met those of the enemy soldier.

Before the enemy could move or shout, a hand snaked out of a dense bush and was clamped over his mouth as his head was jerked back. An arm flashed and Tyme was sure that he could hear the sound of a throat being cut. For a moment there was only a thin line on the skin and then blood blossomed, bursting from the severed arteries and veins, spilling down the front of the man's uniform, staining it crimson. One hand clawed futilely at the air and then dropped.

An instant later Tyme was on his feet, moving toward the first soldier he had seen. He waited until the man stepped from the clearing into the trees, then swept his feet out from under him. The man hit the ground with a grunt, the air forced from his lungs. At that moment Tyme struck, burying his knife in the hollow of the throat, twisting it savagely as he clamped his free hand over the man's mouth.

The man's hands shot up and grabbed Tyme's shirt, dragging it close to his face. The soldier's eyes were on Tyme. They went wide with fright and then seemed to glaze over, staring into the trees. As his grip loosened and his blood stopped spurting, his eyes rolled up into his head. He died with a dry rattling deep in his throat.

Tyme jerked his knife free and spun. Krung stood near the body of the other soldier. He pointed to the rear and Tyme nodded his agreement. He pushed the body of the dead man under the protective leaves of a bush to conceal it. Then he helped Krung hide the first body. He picked up the NVA's ammunition and the weapon and slung it over his shoulder.

Before they retreated to the rest of the team, they watched the clearing and the forest, but saw no sign that anyone else was there. Tyme was convinced that the two men would not be out on their own. In minutes, an hour or two at the most, there would be more enemy soldiers around, hunting them.

When Tyme was sure that no one would appear quickly, he withdrew toward the rest of the team.

Gerber was surprised when Tyme and Krung appeared in front of him. "What happened?" he asked.

"Ran into part of another search party," said Tyme. "Krung killed one and I got the other. Figured there were more of them, but we didn't see anyone."

"Shit!" said Gerber. "I suppose there was no choice in the matter."

"No, sir. The one guy almost stepped on me. Krung had to take him. That meant I had to kill the other one."

"Damn!"

Tyme was crouched on one knee, his rifle in his left hand. He was breathing rapidly, as if he had run the distance back to the team. With his right hand, he wiped the sweat from his face and wiped it on his blood-stained uniform.

"I suspect there are others around," Tyme repeated.

"I agree, Captain," said Fetterman, his voice barely audible. "There are a lot of people out here looking for those downed flyers."

"We could break for the coast," said Gerber. "Our orders are open-ended."

"Or we could try to find the flyers," said Fetterman.

"If we do find them, we might get airlift out. We provide LZ security for the choppers and then hop on when they come in to rescue the pilots," added Bocker.

Gerber hesitated, his eyes roaming the forest. Small, skinny trees, bushes with broad leaves, grass and vines and ferns. A carpeting of wet and decaying leaves. It was possible to see forty, fifty meters in the forest as they moved through it. Very easy for the enemy to spot them.

"Krung, you take the point. Kit, you're right behind him with Fetterman. The rest of us will bring up the rear. Do not engage the enemy unless it is absolutely necessary. Same compass heading as before."

Krung didn't move immediately. He stared at the group with him and then got to his feet. Slowly he stepped between two trees.

A second later Kit was up and moving, following Krung, her rifle held in both hands. As she reached the two trees, she glanced back over her shoulder and nodded to Gerber.

With that, the rest of the team was on their feet, moving among the bushes and trees of the forest. They spread out in a thin line, moving quietly, listening for sounds of pursuit and the sounds of a search party, hoping that they wouldn't stumble over something before nightfall.

12

THE FORESTS SOUTH OF
KE SAT NORTH VIETNAM

At nightfall they stopped long enough to eat a cold meal of tasteless C-rations. Afterward they rested for a moment, and then were up and moving again. Their path meandered to the south and east, avoiding the usual peasant and game trails, villages that weren't marked on the maps, farmers' hootches and open fields. From overhead came the roar of jet aircraft as American air strikes against Hanoi and SAM sites were sent in. They heard the rumble of distant bombs and the popping of the large-caliber antiaircraft weapons.

And even with all that, each was surprised at how deserted the countryside was. Farmers rode in groups to their fields in Soviet-made ZIL trucks and returned to the larger towns at night, apparently afraid of an impending American invasion. There were no lights on because those would provide beacons for the American bombers and fighters.

They avoided one large group of the NVA who had spread out in a clearing, drying themselves in the last of the fading sun. Near the center of the group was a fire under a huge black pot. Three men stood around it, tossing in vegetables and hunks of raw meat. They had stacked their weapons near the cooking pot as they began setting up their camp, apparently planning to stay where they were for the rest of the night.

Once, as Gerber and his team began to move after the evening meal, they heard the distant pop of rotor blades. They knew it was one of the rescue teams searching for downed American flyers. Firing had erupted then. Small arms from the ground and cannons from the fighter escort. It sounded as if the rescue craft had been driven off before they had a chance to pick up the flyers.

Krung, who had been on point, fell to the ground again and waved at Kit, signaling her to the right. Gerber saw the activity and hurried forward.

After a short distance, he dropped to his belly and crawled the rest of the way, being careful not to make noise. Again they were at the edge of a clearing where an NVA unit was spread out. In the center of it were three men. Two of them wore the remains of U.S. Air Force uniforms. The last wore black pajamas and looked as if he had been badly beaten. The flickering firelight played across his features, illuminating them. Gerber felt his stomach turn as he recognized the man in the black pajamas.

Somehow, Le Duc had managed to get himself captured and not executed. Knowing that, Gerber searched the faces of the other two prisoners, but couldn't tell if one of them was Barlett or not. He suspected not because both wore flight uniforms, and not fatigues, but there was no telling for certain. At least it answered one question.

At that moment he felt Fetterman's lips near his ear. "We take them?"

Although he hadn't thought about it, he nodded. "Yeah, we take them. We get Le Duc out of there. I count seven, eight, nine. Nine."

"What's the plan?"

Gerber rolled to his side and looked behind him. In the darkness and shadows of the forest, he could only see one shape. If they spread out and opened fire at the same moment, they could probably kill all the NVA before the enemy could realize what was happening. Tyme or Fetterman could be detailed to take out anyone who reached cover. One of them wouldn't fire with the rest.

As he thought of that, Tyme's words hit him like a rock. Tyme had told him that zeroing the weapons wasn't a luxury and Gerber had forced the issue, telling the weapons specialist that they wouldn't be doing any sniping so that if the sights were off slightly, it wouldn't matter. Now it mattered and there was no way he could go back to zero the weapons. It was the first time that the situation had come up. Maybe it was because they had always zeroed the weapons before the mission. Tyme had always insisted, and had always gotten his way.

Gerber touched Fetterman on the shoulder and pointed twice to the rear and then along the left side of the clearing. Fetterman nodded and retreated to find two people to position there.

Gerber moved closer to Krung and instructed him to wait. He was not to fire until Gerber opened up. Then he was to rake the clearing, being careful not to shoot too low because they didn't want to hit the prisoners seated there.

He positioned the team, instructing them not to open fire until he did and for each to try to kill the enemy soldiers directly in front of them. When they were set, Gerber worked his way back to the center and crouched near the base of a large tree.

He thumbed off the safety and aimed by looking over the top of the barrel, not using the sights because of the darkness. He waited for the NVA soldier in front of him to turn so that he would present his back as a target. Gerber didn't have to wait long. He pulled the trigger, feeling the weapon buck against his shoulder. The smell of burned cordite assailed his nostrils and the green tracers flashed outward, some of them bouncing high.

At that moment the rest of the team began to shoot, pouring rounds into the clearing. Their side of the forest twinkled like Christmas lights from the muzzle flashes. The enemy soldiers fell, shredded by the fusillade. One tried to get up, was struck again and flipped to his back.

When the shooting started, the three prisoners fell facedown. None of them looked up, even after the final shot had been fired. They waited for someone to tell them what to do.

As the echoes faded, Gerber got to his feet. He dropped the empty magazine from his weapon and jammed another one home. He worked the bolt, keeping his eyes on the clearing, his ears cocked, watching the dead men. Finally he pushed himself out of the trees. He stepped to the first body and touched it with the toe of his boot.

The dead man was lying facedown, blood staining the back of his khaki uniform in great wet smears. In the firelight, Gerber could see that part of his face had been blown away by a bullet. The skin along his cheek was ripped, exposing his teeth in a death's head grin. Gerber kicked the AK away from the corpse's outstretched hand.

Around him, the others moved forward, checking the bodies and picking up the weapons. Gerber walked over to the prisoners.

Using his knife, he cut the rough hemp that bound the wrists of the prisoners. ''I'm Captain MacKenzie Gerber, U.S. Army Special Forces.''

One of the Air Force officers sat up and rubbed his wrists. For a moment he said nothing, just stared into the dirty face of the man who had rescued him. Then he grinned. Holding out a hand, he said, "I'm Captain Richard Wornell and I'm happier than hell to see you."

Gerber nodded, looked at the other two men. "You okay, Duc? What the hell happened?"

"NVA got me," said Duc. "They wait for me as I come down. I was all alone and they catch me."

"I can see that. What about Barlett?"

"NVA didn't see him. He ran. They chase and then come back. They say he dead. He fight with them and they kill him. They leave his body for the maggots. But I hear no shooting. Nobody shoot."

"You think he got away, then?" asked Gerber. "You think he's out there on his own?"

"No. I think they catch him and kill him."

"Why?"

"One of them came back with his hat but they don't have him. If they take him alive, they bring him, too, but if they kill him, they leave body."

"What if he managed to get away from them?" insisted Gerber.

"Then they still be out there looking for him, but they came back. I think man dead."

"Captain," said Fetterman, "I think we better get out of here. Someone had to hear the firing."

"Right, Tony." He turned to the Air Force man. "Can you travel?"

"Yes," said Wornell.

"How about your friend?"

"I don't know who he is. We picked him up a day or so after they got me. He hasn't said a word to them. Wouldn't even tell them his name."

"Captain?" said Fetterman.

"Bocker, I want you to stay close to this guy." He pointed to the silent man. To Wornell he said, "Can you use an AK?"

"I know which end the bullets come out of if that's what you mean," he said, his teeth flashing in the firelight.

"Good. Grab a weapon and as much ammo as you can carry. The more the better. Duc, you do the same. As much as you can carry. Tony, let's take some extra weapons with us. You never know when you'll need them. Once we're clear, we'll figure out something else."

Tyme suddenly appeared. "I think someone's coming, Captain. I didn't hang around to get a good count. Sounded like at least a platoon and they didn't give a shit about noise discipline."

Gerber spun toward Fetterman. "Tony, take the point and let's get out of here."

Fetterman grabbed Krung. "Come on."

"Justin, help Captain Wornell and Le Duc. Galvin, let's get going."

"What about me?" asked Kit.

"Follow the rest of them. Go. Go."

Fetterman trotted across the clearing and disappeared into the forest. Krung was right behind him. Tyme gestured at Wornell, pointed him in the right direction and then took off with him. Kit and Le Duc waited for Bocker and the unidentified pilot and followed closely. When everyone was out of sight, Gerber kicked the fire out, spreading the burning embers. Then he, too, ran toward the jungle.

At the edge of the forest he stopped momentarily and looked back. Although he wanted to see if anyone was coming, he couldn't take the chance that he would lose his people. When no one appeared quickly, he spun and ran.

A moment later he found his team as they worked their way through the trees.

He joined them, listening to the noise being made by the Air Force men not familiar with the environment. Heavy footfalls and snapping twigs. Once there was a grunt, as if one of the pilots had walked into a tree.

They kept going for nearly an hour, rushing through the forest, tripping over bushes and logs, disregarding noise discipline as they fell, but afraid to slow the pace. They could hear the pursuers occasionally. They were rattling their equipment, shouting orders to one another, slashing at the vegetation. It was as if they were trying to drive Gerber and his team to panic. Force them to run, forgetting everything they knew. It was a plan that might work against downed pilots, but not men experienced in jungle warfare. It only told Gerber where the enemy was and what he had to do to stay in front of them.

Finally, Gerber decided that they had pressed their luck far enough. He caught up to Fetterman and told him to halt. They spread out, facing opposite directions, listening to the night sounds of the forest around them.

Gerber felt tired. His muscles ached and his mouth was full of cotton. He drank water and offered some of it to Wornell who crouched near him. Wornell took the canteen gratefully and at first sipped the warm water and then chugged it. When he realized that he had swallowed most of it, he handed the canteen back to Gerber and said, rather sheepishly, "Sorry."

"Don't let it bother you."

Fetterman came up and knelt next to Gerber. "Now what, Captain?"

Gerber wanted to look at the map and pinpoint their location. Given anything, he knew that they were south and east of Ke Sat. If he remembered the map correctly, due east was a river system and not far beyond that was the coast, no more than thirty or thirty-five miles. With the Air Force pilots, it could take them a week to travel that far. Without them, they could cover the ground in two days.

"Let's move to the east and try to find a place with good cover, not far from a landing zone. We'll try for a helicopter pickup about dawn."

"Don't need an LZ," said Wornell. "They've got jungle penetrators that can lift us out right through the thickest canopy."

"Captain," said Gerber, "how long does each rescue using the penetrator take? Five minutes? Three? And, of course, there are nine of us. Thirty or forty minutes. Will the chopper hover over the jungle that long?"

"I see your point," said Wornell.

At that moment Tyme approached. He leaned close to Gerber. "I think they're still back there. They're moving quietly now, like they want to catch us unprepared."

"You get an idea of who and how many?"

"No, sir. They're pretty good, though. They're moving rapidly, making little noise now."

"You think we can evade them by hiding?"

"No, sir. I think these guys are going to be poking into bushes and ravines looking for us."

"Okay," said Gerber. "Tony, I want you... No, get Galvin. I'll have him escort the fliers out of here. The rest of us will stay and ambush the enemy patrol."

"Captain," said Fetterman, "I might suggest that Kit go with Galvin. Give him another experienced jungle fighter and someone familiar with the area."

"Okay, Tony. You get the men deployed, and I'll get Galvin and Kit moving."

"Captain," said Wornell, "I know a little about this. Been through a couple of jungle fighting courses with our perimeter defense teams."

"I rarely turn down a volunteer, but this is a little different than that," said Gerber. "Besides, once we spring the ambush, we're going to be moving very fast. You'll be of more use with Sergeant Bocker arranging for that chopper to get us out of here in the morning."

"Yes, sir," said Wornell.

Together they moved to where Bocker crouched, his weapon aimed into the trees, his eyes shifting rapidly. Gerber knelt next to him. "Going to send you ahead with the Air Force people and with Kit. Find a good location for extraction. We'll need an LZ that can accommodate a Sea Stallion, and I'll want a place nearby with good cover. Don't worry about a water source or the like. With luck, we'll be out of here in a couple of hours. The cover is more important now."

"Shouldn't be a major problem," said Bocker.

"Once you've got it established, I want you to make contact with the air-sea rescue boys and arrange extraction for dawn tomorrow. Wornell can help you. We'll have caught up to you by then."

"Yes, sir. When do I go?"

"Now."

Bocker turned and stared into the darkness. He could see the gray shape of Gerber and Wornell. He wanted to look into Wornell's eyes, but it was too dark. Instead he reached out and touched Wornell on the shoulder.

"Let's go."

As they faded into the dark, Gerber moved to the rear. He found Fetterman. "You ready here?"

''Set in an L-shaped ambush. That assumes that they'll be following our trail. Got Tyme in the rear, watching from that direction so that they don't get behind us.''

''Good. Where did you want me?''

''About five meters to the left. Use grenades and once the enemy firing dies down, we'll drop to the rear to wait five minutes. See if they pursue.''

''Then all we can do now is wait.''

''That's about it, sir.''

ROBIN READ THE LAST PAGE of the story, carefully rearranged the papers in their proper order and tapped the edges against the top of the table.

''You can't print this,'' she said.

''Why the hell not?'' demanded George Krupp. ''The facts are accurate.''

Robin stood and moved across the small room to the window. She opened it and looked out on downtown Saigon. She had taken the room because it was cheap, close to her office and gave her a view of the nightclub scene. A contrast that was almost too stark to believe. The countryside was throbbing with war, machine guns and mortars, people dying horribly in filthy rice paddies and dirty villages, yet the downtown looked like any teeming Oriental metropolis in peacetime. Women in revealing costumes and men, many of them in wild civilian clothes, haggling over the prices and services. The glow of the neon radiated up at her, reflecting from the rain-wet streets and the dirty glass of the bars.

''George,'' she said, still staring at the scene below her. ''I don't want to argue about the accuracy of the story. You can't print it because it will endanger the men involved. It gives away too much information.''

"Oh, hell, Robin," he snorted. "That's a load of shit. You going to tell me that the North Vietnamese read the American newspapers? I can't believe Palmer tried to pull that old one on us."

"I just don't see the point in even giving the enemy the opportunity to read about it," she responded.

"I think it's time you found yourself another occupation," said Krupp quietly. "Maybe you've lost your edge here."

"If that means I've developed a sense of responsibility," she said, "then you might be right." She turned to face him. "I've been thinking about this a lot lately. About the role of the press and the power of it, and I think we've gotten too caught up in our own self-importance. Nothing matters except the story and we go after it, claiming the people's right to know, but that's bullshit. We're just after bigger and bigger stories so that we're no longer reporting them, we are them. We've lost our perspective."

"Christ, Robin, those Special Forces jerks have you brainwashed."

She sighed and moved forward to sit on the bed. "No, I don't think that's it. But you know what I mean. I get the big story and suddenly all the other reporters are calling me. I'm interviewed on TV and radio and quoted in the newspaper. I become the source for the story, or I become more important than the story."

"There's nothing wrong with that," said Krupp. "It's merely the recognition you deserve for finding a good story. For ferreting out facts and information that everyone else would prefer that you didn't have."

Robin shook her head. "Not when I decide that I know what's best for everyone. Not when I claim that the people have a right to know while endangering the lives of others. People who have the right to live."

"I still say it's a load of shit." He grabbed his story off the table. "I'm going to file it because the people do have a right to know. They have the right to know that their government is trying to get them involved in a land war with nearly a billion Chinese. One that could easily escalate into a global, thermonuclear war."

"You talk about me slinging the shit. You've taken the story of some downed crewmen and changed it into the possibility of nuclear war." She laughed humorlessly. "You see. You're doing exactly what I've said. Taken a nothing story and changed into the end of the human race. And you don't care about the men in North Vietnam fighting for their lives."

"I have no interest in them. I don't know them and I doubt my story could hurt them."

"And if you knew it would? Then what?"

"That's a ridiculous question, Robin."

She stared up at him, not sure that she liked what she saw. Afraid that she saw herself reflected in the man. Chase the story and to hell with the consequences. She knew that wasn't right because she had withheld one hell of a story to protect the people involved. And then she wondered if she would have done it if she hadn't been in love with one of the principal men in it.

"What difference is a day or two going to matter?" asked Robin. "By waiting a day or two, you might be able to write the end to the story. A much better end."

"In a day or two I will write the end to it, but now I'm going to file this one."

"Somehow I knew you were going to say that."

13

**THE FOREST REGION
EAST AND SOUTH OF KE
SAT NORTH VIETNAM**

Bocker found the perfect place in less than thirty minutes. The hilltop, no higher than fifty feet above the rest of the territory, was hidden from the rice paddies and farm fields surrounding it by the trees that grew halfway up the slope. The top was lightly grassed, nearly a hundred feet across, and would easily hold a Sea Stallion. If there were enemy soldiers standing in the rice paddies, they would not be able to see the hilltop because of the trees.

The forest was thick in places and thin in others. There were a few outcroppings of rock, ravines hidden by bushes and grass, and a few trails. From the summit, they could command a view of all approaches. The forest would inhibit the enemy, holding him back if he tried to rush the hilltop as the chopper landed on it.

After climbing partway up, he detoured to the south and found a hiding place there. He put the uncommunicative flier in the center of a rocky fort with Wornell, Kit and himself guarding him. In the half light of the moon and the ground glow from rotting vegetation, Bocker could see remarkably well. It always surprised him how bright the night could be when the moon was nearly full and the stars were blazing.

He slipped into position, checked the likely avenues of attack. Satisfied there'd be no threat, he leaned close to Wornell. "Think you can raise the rescue boys on your radio?"

"I can give it a try. What do you want?"

"Captain said to get a chopper in here about dawn. Land and pick us up. You can arrange that. Tell them about us, too. We don't want to get mistaken for NVA. Tell them that we'll have secured the LZ so they won't have to worry about a bunch of NVA showing up."

"I doubt that'll bother them. They'll have fighter escort to take care of any ground threat."

"You work on getting that arranged then."

"Okay, Sergeant."

With that, Bocker stole back to the man who hadn't spoken. He performed the best examination that he could under the circumstances, and found no obvious wounds. The man's limbs seemed intact, devoid of breaks. As he worked on him he noticed a name tag and leaned close to it. Even in the half light of the moon and stars, he could read the name. McMaster.

Bocker sat back on his heels, looked into McMaster's eyes. "Captain McMaster, I'm Sergeant Galvin Bocker, United States Army Special Forces. You're safe with us now. The enemy won't be able to get to you."

McMaster didn't respond. He stared straight ahead, as if he was catatonic. When Kit approached, McMaster turned to stare at her, but didn't speak.

"Is he all right?" she asked.

Bocker nodded and heard the first burst of firing from the west, a high-pitched, staccato sound that punctuated the night. It sounded like a single AK on full auto. Then came the dull thuds as grenades exploded. One. Two. A half dozen, and then more firing of AKs. In seconds it was over. Silence.

Bocker searched the area to his right, where the sound of the battle had come from, but could see nothing. He wished he could head in that direction to offer assistance, but knew what his orders were. Instead he listened to the growing silence and prayed that the ambush had worked, that it had been Gerber and Fetterman and his men who had been successful. Who had survived.

TYME HAD BEEN RIGHT about the NVA unit chasing them. They were very good. Gerber could hear almost nothing. Only the occasional scrape of a boot against the exposed root of a tree, or a dull, quiet clink as metal touched metal. They were moving slowly now.

Then he saw the first of the enemy soldiers. A dark shape moving among the trees. Even in the night he could see the telltale shape of an AK-47 held at high port, the flattened pith helmet the enemy wore and the chest pouch for spare AK-47 magazines. The man's head swiveled right and left as he searched both sides of the trail, looking for signs of the men they were chasing.

Several soldiers followed that man. They had spread out in a loose triangle-shaped formation. A few had the bayonets on their weapons extended and were using them to prod the bushes as they passed them.

At that moment there was a burst of AK fire. A stream of emerald-colored tracers lashed through the night. Two of the men toppled into the bushes, one of them screaming in pain.

"Grenades!"

Gerber jerked the pin from his grenade and threw it at one of the enemy soldiers. He snatched a second and repeated the performance. Then he dropped flat, his hands over his ears to protect them from the shock waves of the detonations.

There was a series of explosions. Crashes that shattered the night. Fiery bursts lit up large sections of the trail, freezing the action. Shrapnel rattled overhead, smashing into the trees, shredding them and tearing the leaves off the branches. The debris rained down gently, quietly. Gerber rolled to the right and poked the barrel of his weapon out in front of him.

The night was ripped by more firing from AKs. Muzzle flashes winked as the tongues of flame leaped out of the barrels. Green and white tracers lanced outward and bounced high. They crisscrossed in the night. Gerber used his own weapon to hose down the area.

"Fall back!" he ordered. "Fall back!"

With that, he was on his feet, moving rapidly through trees, heading to the rear. He spotted Fetterman and angled toward him. "Take the point."

Fetterman turned and ran into the trees. Krung and Le Duc were behind him. Gerber hesitated, saw Tyme and pointed at the others. Tyme spun, emptied his magazine into the forest where the enemy was. Then he dropped back. As he ran he changed the magazine in his weapon, letting the empty fall to the forest floor. Away from the ambush site, he fell into line. When he was sure that all his men were away safely, Gerber took off after them.

They ran through the forest, popped into the clear and kept on running. They crossed the area, splashing through a couple of rice paddies, and then entered the forest on the other side. As he got to the trees he found Fetterman deploying the troops again.

"Good place to stop the pursuit." The breath was rasping in Fetterman's throat.

Gerber glanced over his shoulder and saw the moonlight reflecting off the dirty water. The area was wide open and would provide little cover for the North Vietnamese. There was a network of low dikes and then the black smudge that was the forest opposite them.

"Yeah," he agreed. "We can catch our breath, but if we see no sign of the enemy in fifteen minutes, we take off. We don't want to wait for them to find us."

Gerber dropped to the ground. Through a gap in the vegetation in front of him, he had a perfect view of the clearing. Sweat popped out on his forehead and dripped down the sides of his face. He touched his forehead to his shoulder to dab away the sweat, afraid to rub it because it might remove the camouflage paint. He worked hard so that his breathing wasn't an audible rasp but a quiet intake of air.

The time passed slowly. Gerber kept looking at his watch and then glancing right and left, at the men with him. Suddenly in front of him, at the far edge of the clearing, he thought he caught a flicker of movement. He studied the black mass of trees, and saw it again. Movement just inside the tree line.

"Here they come," he hissed. "Let them get into the open before firing."

The enemy seemed to hover inside the forest, as if they knew what was going on, and then slipped out of the trees. Two men on point cautiously entered the clearing. They separated, moved to one of the dikes and crouched near it. More men emerged from the trees, moving hunched over, their weapons held at port arms.

As they fanned out, the flankers, separated from the main body by ten or twelve meters, appeared. They approached the point men, slowing down as they did so. The point got up, sweeping forward.

When they were halfway across the field, Gerber used his last grenade. He tossed it as far as he could, aiming for a point beyond the NVA soldiers. There was a quiet splash, like a fish breaking water. A couple of the enemy turned, searching behind them as the grenade exploded into a flash of light that silhouetted them.

Before the enemy could dive for cover or retreat into the forest, Gerber's men opened fire. The night was filled with the rattle of rifle fire, the tracers bouncing as they struck the ground.

The enemy panicked. Two of them ran into the blazing barrels of the American weapons. They were cut down quickly, their bodies disappearing into the filthy water.

The main body of NVA soldiers returned fire quickly. The rounds snapped through the leaves over the Americans' heads and slammed into the trunks of the trees with dull thuds. The strobing lights of the muzzles gave away their locations.

"Grenades!" ordered Fetterman.

A second later there were two explosions and then a third. Return fire from the enemy stopped abruptly. A few random shots echoed among the trees, then there was complete silence. Gerber pulled the empty magazine from his weapon, tossed it away and slammed a fresh one home.

For a few minutes they waited, searching for signs of movement, but there were none. Apparently everyone had either been killed or had managed to reach the trees without being seen. Gerber knew he should check the field, but didn't want to expose his men to enemy fire. He would have to leave things as they stood.

He crawled away from the edge of the clearing, and found Fetterman. Touching the master sergeant on the back, he whispered, "Let's get out of here."

They alerted the rest of the men and then, keeping low, they withdrew. Once clear of the area, they got up and began moving faster. Fetterman remained at the rear, watching and listening for signs of pursuit.

It wasn't long before they came to the hillside. Gerber called a halt, then sent Tyme out in search of Bocker. In a few moments, the whole team was united.

"What happened?" he asked.

"We got them," said Tyme, his voice quiet but filled with excitement.

"I've got a good hiding place over there," said Bocker. Without another word, he led them to it.

Once inside the rock enclosure, Gerber asked, "You have any luck making contact with the rescue choppers?"

Wornell spoke up. "They'll be here at first light. Claimed they got a good fix on my signal and were satisfied with the recognition and authentication codes I gave them."

"Thanks." Gerber moved closer to Fetterman. "After that ambush, they're going to be beating the ground for us tonight."

"Maybe not," said Fetterman.

"We've been lucky," said Gerber. "We got in and out of the missile site with no casualties. We've had a couple of run-ins and left bodies scattered all over but not run into any real trouble yet. They're going to be looking for us."

"Yes, sir," said Fetterman, "but I don't think they'll do anything until the morning. Every time they've gone up against us in the dark we've zapped them."

"I was thinking," said Gerber. "Maybe you and Tyme could slip back along our trail and rig a mechanical ambush. It would slow down their pursuit."

"I'll get Justin and we'll do it."

Tyme and Fetterman, carrying several of the spare
weapons, extra magazines and the majority of the remain-
ing grenades, worked their way down the hill. They moved
rapidly, avoiding the paths as they walked through the forest. They reached the bottom of the hill. Fetterman stopped
for a moment, surveying the area around them.

There were a couple of likely approaches from the west.
A wide path led toward the crest of the hill and he also noticed a couple of smaller, less well-defined trails. If the enemy was going to approach, he figured they would use the
paths because there was no reason for them not to. Am-
bushes and booby traps were not that common in the
North, so the soldiers there had not learned to avoid them.

Fetterman told Tyme to take some of the equipment and
rig it to cover the paths. When the younger man disappeared into the forest, Fetterman set to work.

First he took one of the AKs and wired it into the fork of
a tree so that it was pointing to the west, covering the path.
He looped the wire through the trigger guard and tied it
with a slip knot. He then hooked it around the butt of the
weapon, fastened it under a forked stick shoved into the
earth and played it out across the trail. He anchored it there,
tying it around the base of a sapling. Before he left, he made
sure that the wire was taut. If someone's boot struck the
wire, it would tighten the loop around the trigger, causing
the weapon to fire. The whole thirty-round magazine would
empty, raking the trail with 7.62 mm ammunition.

That finished, he moved farther to the west and set an
empty C ration can on the ground. With his knife, he buried the can and anchored it with a couple of small sticks.
He tied the end of his wire around the top of the grenade
and stuffed it into the can. Again he stretched the wire
across the trail, making sure that it was only two or three

inches above the dirt. When someone kicked it, the grenade would be jerked from the can and would explode.

He returned to the can, took the grenade from it and pulled the pin. Carefully he slipped it back into the tin. When the grenade was yanked from the can now, with the pin out, the safety spoon would fly off.

Fetterman spent the next hour rigging other surprises. Some of them were little more than punji stakes, sharpened bits of bamboo hidden in shallow, camouflaged holes or set on traps that would sweep across the trail knee high or crotch high. He didn't have much faith in those, but they would be enough to slow down the enemy, if they were getting close. A man looking for booby traps in addition to fleeing soldiers moved slower than a man just chasing the enemy.

He rigged a second booby trap with an AK, this set at crotch level. He tied the barrel down carefully so that it wouldn't rise as the weapon burned through the magazine. Finally satisfied with his preparations, he moved to the rear, looking for Tyme.

The young weapons specialist had set up a dual AK arrangement. The first one was set to be tripped by someone walking on the trail, catching the wire with his foot. As it fired, the recoil of the weapon was set so that it tightened the wire on the second AK. If he had calculated correctly, the first weapon would be about halfway through the magazine when the second, aimed lower, would begin to fire. It would appear to be two soldiers shooting from two locations. It would take the enemy several minutes to discover the nature of the trap. Those could be the minutes the Americans needed to escape.

He had also rigged a couple of grenade traps, including one set so that the grenade, as it was pulled from the can, would be jerked upward and explode five or six feet in the air. The burst would throw the shrapnel about head high and none of it would be wasted as it was in a ground explosion.

Convinced that they had done everything they could, they withdrew from the area, trying to cover the evidence of the booby traps, but leaving some sign that they had been there; those footprints, bent twigs and crushed blades of grass would lead the enemy into trap. If the enemy panicked, they could spend an hour trying to figure it out.

Together, they worked their way back to where the rest of the team waited. They were challenged, quietly, but Bocker recognized them and gave them the word to approach. Gerber was waiting there. "You see anyone?"

Fetterman shook his head. "Nothing. If they're moving in on us, they're doing it quietly and carefully."

Gerber pulled back the camouflage band on his watch. "Be light in another hour or so."

"Yes, sir. I would think anyone out there would be following our path closely. That being the case, if they're reading the signs we left, they'll walk into the ambush. That'll warn us they're close."

"And give us a chance to escape," said Gerber.

"But I don't think they'll be looking for us before morning. The night is our ally. They'll probably regroup near that last ambush and then sweep out from there. In the daylight we're at the disadvantage."

"I think you're right, Tony. Let's spread out a little more and keep our eyes open. With any luck, we'll be out of here long before the enemy can get close to us."

Dawn broke quietly. A mist obscured the clearing and hid the trees on the other side of it. Fetterman and Tyme scouted the trees, making sure that no one had sneaked up on them during the night.

Bocker and Wornell crouched among the rocks, the antenna of the survival radio up. For a few minutes they listened to the frequency but heard nothing. Bocker shrugged. "Go ahead."

"Rescue, this is Baron One."

"Baron One, this is Kingfisher Two-Two. Say authentication number."

"Zero-six-one-two."

"Authentication confirmed. Say condition."

"Be advised that there are ten of us now. Condition is good."

"Enemy troops?"

"No contact with the enemy for nearly four hours. LZ is secure."

"Roger. We are inbound. Wait, One."

The radio went silent and Bocker looked at Wornell, who raised an eyebrow in question. Bocker shrugged. He wasn't familiar with the procedures used by the air-sea rescue people this far north.

"Baron One, we will be at your location in one-five minutes. Do you have smoke?"

Bocker nodded his head vigorously.

"Roger, we have smoke."

Gerber moved toward them, "Let's head up the hill. Galvin take the point and don't get sloppy now. We're too close to getting out."

They formed a single-file column with the still silent pilot, McMaster, in the center. Bocker leaped over the rocks, knelt there for a moment as if waiting for someone to start shooting at him and then began a rapid climb up the rest of the hill.

The terrain wasn't bad. They could use the saplings to haul themselves up the hillside. The carpet of decaying vegetation, wet with the early-morning dew, kept the noise down. The slanting rays of the early-morning sun illuminated the forest around them. There were some mature trees and full-grown bushes, but quite a bit of younger vegetation.

In only a few minutes they had reached the edge of the trees at the top of the hillside. Wornell dropped to the ground, his back to a tree, relaxing. Bocker turned, hesitating, waiting for instructions from Gerber.

"Let's not fall apart now," he said. As Fetterman approached, Gerber pointed and said, "Tony. Security right and left."

"Yes, sir."

Fetterman moved to the right and Tyme headed in the opposite direction. Gerber slid down the hillside for twenty feet and found a shallow depression. He lay in it, concealing himself, and kept his eyes downslope, searching for the enemy.

Glancing at his watch, he decided that the enemy wouldn't have time to find them now. In minutes they would be airborne, flying out of North Vietnam, the mission halfway completed. He regretted that he couldn't get into the Hanoi Hilton, but that instruction had been stupid. With his small force he would never have been able to get clear. Perhaps with the element of surprise they could get in easily, but within minutes they would have been trapped. Still, it was an interesting prospect.

The air overhead was split by the sound of a low-flying jet. Gerber looked up and through gaps in the trees, saw the smoky trail of a Phantom. He grinned, knowing that the choppers couldn't be far behind.

At that moment the first of the booby traps in the mechanical ambush went off. There was the detonation of a grenade and then the ripping blast of an AK. Silence fell and then the cacophony rose again as the enemy soldiers tried to return fire. First there was only a couple of their weapons, and then more as all the enemy began to return the fire until it sounded like a company was closing in on them.

Around him, Gerber could hear the stray rounds ripping through the trees over his head, peeling bark from the trunks, and tearing leaves from the branches. He hesitated, watching the slope below, but nothing moved down there. Then, in the distance he heard the heavy pop of the rotor blades of the Sea Stallion. Jet engines roared, nearly drowning out the sounds of shooting.

Gerber got to his feet and ran up the slope. He came to Fetterman and pointed. Fetterman and Tyme took up the rear guard position, their weapons ready, as Bocker and Wornell ran to the center of the LZ.

Wornell dropped to the ground and pulled at the antenna of his radio. He pointed it straight up and said, "This is Baron One."

"Roger, Baron One. Can you pop smoke?"

Bocker took a smoke grenade from his pack, pulled the pin and tossed it to the center of the LZ. A yellow cloud began to billow.

Kit, Krung and Le Duc gathered near a tall tree. At first they watched Bocker and Wornell, and then turned to where Gerber, Fetterman and Tyme crouched. Krung moved closer to the Special Forces men, his weapon held ready. He heard Kit whisper at him, but waved a hand to silence her without turning around.

Through the trees, Gerber caught movement. A shape flashed and then fell. He kept his eyes turned toward it, and saw it begin to crawl forward. Gerber aimed, but didn't fire.

A grenade exploded. Gerber saw the flash and then the drifting cloud of dust. More firing erupted as the enemy soldiers fired into the trees, as if they believed they had been surrounded. More grenades exploded, but these were duller, quiet pops. The NVA were throwing their own grenades, trying to break up the ambush.

Behind the Special Forces men the roar of the jets came again and then the popping rotors became louder. Gerber looked over his shoulder, saw the yellow cloud drifting on the center of the LZ and knew that the chopper was inbound.

"Let's take them," he said.

With that, he let the front sight seek the enemy soldier. As soon as he saw the movement again, he pulled the trigger, felt the weapon slam back into his shoulder. The man took the round in the side of the head. For a moment he was frozen there, a gaping red wound between his eye and ear. Then he slowly collapsed.

Both Fetterman and Tyme opened fire on full auto. They burned through the ammo as fast as they could, changing magazines without hesitation. Their rounds tore through the thin vegetation, shredding the trunks of the saplings and ripping the leaves from bushes.

Return fire was sporadic and poorly aimed. The enemy was thoroughly confused, firing in all directions. They seemed to be pinned down by the mechanical ambush. Gerber watched the shooting, and tried to spot the muzzle flashes, but the rising sun washed them out.

He began to crawl toward the rear until he found Fetterman. Gerber ordered the master sergeant to collect Tyme and follow. Then he located another good hiding position and dropped into it.

Fetterman and Tyme rushed by. Fetterman halted, spun and emptied his weapon into the forest. He dropped to one knee, jerked his last grenade from his pistol belt and tossed it into the trees. Then he ran into the clearing.

Gerber waited for the grenade to explode. When he saw the orange flash and the fountain of dirt and debris raining back to the ground, Gerber was on his feet, running.

As he passed the last of the trees, he saw the chopper coming out of the sun, right at him. It was a gigantic machine, capable of carrying forty troops. Behind it were two jet fighters, patrolling, looking for the enemy, waiting for the Triple A to open fire.

Gerber slipped to one knee and aimed his weapon at the trees. Fetterman and Tyme ran toward him, and fell next to him, but none of them fired.

The noise increased until it was a roar that overpowered everything else. The rotor wash blew with the force of a small hurricane, trying to smash them to the ground. The swirling wind grabbed at them, ripping at them and tearing at the loose grass, leaves and debris in the LZ. It threw up a whirling cloud of dust, sucked the last of the yellow smoke in, and tossed it out.

Behind him, Bocker and Wornell scrambled toward the open door on the right side of the chopper. Wornell leaped into the interior and rolled against the bulkhead. Kit dropped her rifle, stooped to pick it up and then fell to her knees. From the trees, to the right of where Gerber had been, an RPD opened fire, stitching the side of the chopper. Kit snatched her weapon from the grass, spun and emptied the magazine at the machine-gun nest.

Firing around them increased. Gerber was on his feet, running. He saw Fetterman shooting. Duc was aiming into the trees where the RPD was concealed and Gerber yelled at him. "On the chopper! Get on the chopper!"

As Duc turned to run, a round caught him in the shoulder, spinning him to the ground. His weapon flew from his hands and he screamed once. It was a sharp, piercing sound that was nearly lost in the roar of the jets and throbbing of the Sea Stallion's rotor blades.

Gerber grabbed Duc under the other arm and jerked him to his feet. Duc took a stumbling step, caught his balance and ran. At the chopper, Bocker grabbed him around the waist and threw him inside.

Both Fetterman and Tyme were shooting now, pouring rounds into the forest, aiming at the RPD. It fell silent as the NVA gunners dived for cover. Then the two Americans were on their feet, running toward the Sea Stallion.

Gerber reached the chopper but didn't climb in. He stood, his rifle at his shoulder, and when two enemy soldiers appeared, he opened up. Both dived to the side. As they did, Fetterman and Tyme reached the helicopter. They scrambled up. Kit still had not entered. She was now next to Gerber, shooting at anything that moved.

''Get in! Go!''

She didn't move. She kept pulling the trigger until the bolt locked back.

Gerber saw that and slapped at her. She glared at him as Bocker grabbed her under the arms, throwing her up into the chopper.

At that moment Gerber tossed his weapon through the hatch. He reached out, grabbed the side and lifted. Bocker held a helping hand out and a crewman snatched at Gerber, dragging him partially inside.

Before he could get fully on board, the chopper lifted off. It climbed straight up while Gerber held on, his feet waving in midair. He felt his hand slip and was sure that he was going to fall, but then others grabbed him, jerking him into the cabin. The chopper spun, dived at the trees to pick up speed.

From below came the sound of the enemy weapons. An RPD, AKs and even SKS carbines. There were snaps and pops as rounds penetrated the thin metallic skin of the chopper. Then came a single, loud explosion as one of the covering jets began suppressing fire. Gerber looked back and saw the edge of the tree line engulfed in flames, black smoke billowing into the sky.

"We get everyone?" shouted Gerber. He looked around, trying to make a head count.

"Everyone's out," Bocker yelled, nodding with an exaggerated motion. "We got everyone out."

Gerber relaxed leaning against the metal of a bulkhead. He looked at the dirty, sweating faces of the men around him and felt his stomach turn over. Those last, hectic minutes had done it. He could feel the excitement bubbling through him, coursing through his veins. He wanted to shout, to scream, but knew he was premature. They were still over North Vietnam.

Then, through the door of the chopper he saw the tan sand of a beach and the blue green of the Gulf of Tonkin. The chopper continued to climb as two F-4 Phantoms shot by, one of them doing a barrel roll.

At that moment, he knew they were clear.

14

THE CARASEL HOTEL
SAIGON

Mack Gerber sat at a table in the corner of the bar outside the hotel. A copy of *Stars and Stripes* lay in front of him. He had been back from North Vietnam for nearly a week, but because of all the briefings and debriefings, he hadn't gotten to the hotel until earlier that morning. His first act was to take a long, hot shower and then to dress in the wildest civilian clothes he had. A Hawaiian shirt covered with blue birds and red flowers and purple volcanos. He wore bright yellow pants and frayed black tennis shoes without socks.

Across the table from him, Robin Morrow sat quietly sipping the beer he had bought her. Her low-cut dress revealed the tops of her breasts, and the hemline came almost to mid-thigh. She was uncomfortable, the sweat beading on her forehead and upper lip, dampening her hair, but she said nothing about it. She was happy to be with Gerber without having to worry about the Vietnamese woman they all now called Kit, or Fetterman or George Krupp or even Jerry Maxwell and the rest of the CIA spooks.

Gerber folded back the front page of the *Stars and Stripes*, punched in the gutter to flatten it, and was surprised to see a story by George Krupp and Robin Morrow that detailed illegal operations in North Vietnam by members of the U.S. Army's Special Forces. He glanced over the top of the paper at Morrow, who was looking over the railing around the perimeter of the outside bar, staring into the streets of Saigon.

He scanned the story quickly, wondering what asshole had leaked it. He figured it had to be Maxwell or one of the civilians in the embassy who refused to understand that the North Vietnamese routinely violated the supposed neutrality of Laos and Cambodia, and who had large numbers of troops fighting in the South.

With that, the memories of the debriefings returned. Gerber, Fetterman, Tyme and Bocker, had sat in the cold conference rooms. An almost endless parade of military officers and civilian intelligence experts had filed through asking questions. They believed that Gerber and his men deserved no consideration and owed the debriefers something other than honest answers.

First there had been the three men, Robert Cornett, General Thomas Christie and Tim Underwood. They had spent several hours going over every detail of the SAM missile site near Ke Sat. They had been appalled that Gerber had not explored the base at greater length, especially when the missiles on the launchers were found to be dummies but the radar and tracking vans had been real.

Gerber had tried to explain that the North Vietnamese Army hadn't been thrilled to have Gerber and his team running around on the site. Besides, the longer he thought about it, the more he was convinced that he had seen everything that needed to be seen. He had all the answers to the questions. It was only a case of analyzing the data to learn exactly what it all meant.

Cornett had been interested in Fetterman's find of SA-7s and as Gerber thought about it, everything began to make sense. It was what Gerber had suspected all along, but a suspicion that he had failed to voice.

A jet pilot, seeing a missile launch in the dark from an SA-2 site, while flying below two or three hundred feet, would assume the missile launched was an SA-2. At night he would only have the rocket flame and site configuration to give him a missile ID. With less than two seconds to identify the missile and to evade it, the assumption would be that it was an SA-2. After all, one bright flash from a missile engine igniting looked pretty much like the next. The split second that the pilots had to react made their observations of flight characteristics of the missile less than perfect.

"Then that's it," shouted Christie. "The SA-7 is an infrared guided missile. They use the Spoon Rest for early acquisition, get a flight heading and then shut it all down. No SAM warning lights for the aircraft as the North Vietnamese soldiers grab their weapons and suddenly the fucking missiles are coming up at our boys."

Underwood nodded slowly. "And we are led to believe they've added something new to their inventory. Something we can't counter so we stop the bombing raids." He clapped his hands. "A marvelously constructed plan."

Bocker looked confused and then asked, "What's going on here?"

Gerber waited but no one else spoke. "The new guidance system that everyone was so worried about doesn't exist." He stared Christie in the eyes and added, "General, I believe your pilots' debriefings need to be a bit more detailed. The observable characteristics of the SA-7 vary significantly from the SA-2."

"That's right, Captain," said Christie. "We've done everything we can, but when you're flying over an SA-2 site and you have a missile coming at you, you're usually so busy trying to evade it, you don't have time to study it. The assumption is that it was an SA-2."

"I understand that, General," said Gerber. "But it was my butt hanging out in North Vietnam because your people misread the situation."

"Actually, *Captain*," said Christie, stressing Gerber's lower rank, "it was the CIA and Naval Intelligence people who leaped to the wrong conclusions. They followed their guidelines. Before we initiated the activity, that is, your mission into North Vietnam, we would have spent a little more time studying the situation."

"Yes, sir," said Gerber. "But that didn't keep my people out of the North, did it?"

And when the Air Force and CIA had finished with them, Army Intelligence came in, asking for everything that they could get. Unit organizations, uniforms, training, equipment and morale they had seen of the North Vietnamese Army. Did it seem that the NVA was getting ragged, sloppy? Did it seem that discipline was about to break down? Gerber, Fetterman, Tyme and Bocker had told them everything they could remember. In the end the Army people went away very happy.

Finally there was an Air Force contingent that wanted to know what happened to Barlett. This was the debriefing that Gerber had dreaded because no one had a good answer. Le Duc had reported that Barlett had been captured or killed before he had gotten very far off the LZ. Gerber speculated that Barlett, because he wasn't used to the military chutes and all the ramifications of a combat HALO operation, had popped his chute early and drifted a long way from the rest of them. Separated in hostile territory, he had been either captured or killed. But Gerber, knowing that the Air Force would want to protect the memory of their own, told the Air Force investigators that Barlett had been a brave man and had gone down fighting. There was no point in telling them that Barlett had been a big pain in the butt and probably would have compromised the mission within hours.

"And there was nothing you could do for him?" asked the Air Force officer when Gerber had finished his speculation about Barlett.

"We had no idea where he was or if he was alive until we located Le Duc. We were on another mission, which had priority. Once we found Le Duc, it became obvious that Sergeant Barlett had been killed in action."

When the Air Force officer left, there was a final debriefing with the air rescue people about the procedures used. And finally, with a word of caution from Jerry Maxwell to keep their mouths shut about the mission to North Vietnam, they were released. No one asked why they didn't try to break into the Hanoi Hilton or why they didn't make more of an effort to find the downed aircrews. And no one wondered why they hadn't tried to get to one of the other missile sites to examine the weapons there. Gerber assumed that it was because the requests were seen for what they had been. Pipe dreams at best and disasters at worst.

Now, sitting across from Robin, the late afternoon sun beating down on him and making him squint, he felt the anger boil up inside him. They had gone through all that. Men had died for the information they had gotten, and Robin had tried to blow it all. If the story had appeared any earlier, it could have compromised the whole mission, jeopardizing all their lives.

He folded the paper and tossed it across the table at her. "You really responsible for this piece of shit?"

She glanced at the paper. "Not really."

"Your name is on it."

"Right. George thought he was doing me a favor by adding my name to the byline."

"You realize that this kind of irresponsible reporting can get men killed."

She felt the anger flare in her and then burst. After all she had gone through with Krupp, Maxwell and the others, she didn't like his attitude. "I don't need a lecture from you on the workings of the press."

"Somebody sure as hell does. Somebody needs to rein these guys in."

"Not me. I got the story held up for a week as it was. I told George all about responsible journalism and that in time of war some things had to be soft-pedaled. But do you give me credit for half a brain? Oh no. You immediately assume that I've done it again. You don't even have the courtesy to ask. You just assume the worst. After all I've been through for you, after all the crap I've taken as you chase my sister or that Vietnamese whore, I still come back for more. I must be stupid."

Gerber rocked back in his chair and stared at her. The venom of her response surprised him. He had assumed that everything was fine between them when he had gone off on his merry way. Well, maybe not exactly fine. He realized that she wasn't angry about his accusation. It was something more than that and he understood it now.

He had the sense not to try to jolly her out of it. Instead he leaned closer and took hold of one of her unyielding hands. "I'm sorry Robin, I didn't know..."

"How could you not know?" she asked, her voice breaking. "After everything, how could you not know?"

"Incredible stupidity on my part. It's not much, but maybe you'll be happy to know that Karen is madder than hell at me.'' He stopped speaking, his mind running full speed. Suddenly it was important to him that she understand what was going on. ''She found out that I sneaked into Vietnam behind her back. Claimed that it was just an excuse to dump her, and pretended that she didn't know that it was coming. Said she never wanted to see me again. She was breaking it off.''

Robin smiled weakly. ''She was breaking it off? Is that what she said?''

''Well, she was a tad late, but that was what she said.''

''You won't go crawling back to her?''

''No, Robin, I won't.'' He felt her hand soften and then grip his.

''And you understand about the story? That it wasn't my fault?''

''The press is doing more to undermine our effort here than everything the VC and North Vietnamese can throw at us. You have to understand my reaction to a story like that one.'' Even as he said it, he knew Robin wasn't interested in that. They were talking on two different levels but it was all about one thing. It was about them.

''Yes, but after all we've been through, you should know I wouldn't do a thing like that,'' she said.

Gerber knew she was right. With his free hand, he grabbed his beer and drained the glass. He set it down, and then got to his feet.

''Come on,'' he said, ''I want to talk about this somewhere a little more private.''

For a moment she resisted him, pulling at his hand. ''Discuss this? Private?''

''You know perfectly well what I mean.''

She stood, knowing perfectly well what he meant and approving of it completely.

GLOSSARY

AC—An aircraft commander. The pilot in charge of the aircraft.

AK-47—Assault rifle normally used by the North Vietnamese and the Vietcong.

AO—Area of Operations.

AP ROUNDS—Armor-piercing ammunition.

APU—Auxiliary Power Unit. An outside source of power used to start aircraft engines.

ARVN—Army of the Republic of Vietnam. A South Vietnamese soldier. Also known as Marvin Arvin.

BISCUIT—Term that refers to C-rations.

BODY COUNT—The number of enemy killed, wounded or captured during an operation. Used by Saigon and Washington as a means of measuring progress of the war.

BOOM BOOM—Term used by the Vietnamese prostitutes in selling their product.

BOONDOGGLE—Any military operation that hasn't been completely thought out. An operation that is ridiculous.

BOONIE HATS—A soft cap worn by the grunts in the field when not wearing their steel pot.

BUSHMASTER—A jungle warfare expert or soldier skilled in jungle navigation. Also a large deadly snake not common to Vietnam but mighty tasty.

C AND C—The Command and Control aircraft that circles overhead to direct combined air and ground operations.

CARIBOU—Cargo transport plane.

CHINOOK—Army Aviation twin-engine helicopter. A CH-47. Also known as a shit hook.

CHOCK—Refers to the number of the aircraft in the flight. Chock Three is the third, Chock Six is the sixth.

CLAYMORE—An antipersonnel mine that fires 750 steel balls with a lethal range of 50 meters.

CLOSE AIR SUPPORT—Use of airplanes and helicopters to fire on enemy units near friendlies.

CO CONG—A female Vietcong.

C-RATS—C-rations.

DAI UY—Vietnamese Army rank the equivalent of captain.

DEROS—Date Estimated Return from Overseas.

ELEMENT—Two aircraft working together. Two elements or more make up a flight.

EWO—Electronic Warfare Officer.

FEET WET—Term used by pilots to describe flight over water.

FIVE—Radio call sign for the executive officer of a unit.

FOX MIKE—FM radio.

FNG—A fucking new guy.

FREEDOM BIRD—Name given to any aircraft that takes troops out of Vietnam. Usually refers to the commercial jet flights that take men back to the World.

GARAND—The M-1 rifle was replaced by the M-14. Issued to the Vietnamese early in the war.

GO-TO-HELL RAG—Towel or any large cloth worn around the neck by grunts.

GRAIL—The NATO name for the shoulder-fired SA-7 surface-to-air missile.

GUARD THE RADIO—A term that means to stand by in the commo bunker and listen for messages.

GUIDELINE—The NATO term for the SA-2 surface-to-air missiles.

GUNSHIP—Armed helicopter or cargo plane that carries weapons instead of cargo.

HALO—High Altitude Low Opening. A type of parachute jump.

HE—High-explosive ammunition.

HOOTCH—Almost any shelter, from temporary to long-term.

HORN—Term that refers to a specific kind of radio operation that uses satellites to rebroadcast messages.

HORSE—See Biscuit.

HOTEL THREE—A helicopter landing area at Saigon's Ton Son Nhut Airport.

HUEY—A UH-1 helicopter.

ILS—Instrument Landing System.

IN-COUNTRY—Term used to refer to American troops operating in South Vietnam. They were all in-country.

INTELLIGENCE—Any information about enemy operations. It can include troop movements, weapons, capabilities, biographies of enemy commanders, and general information about terrain features. Any information that would be useful in planning a mission.

KABAR—A type of military combat knife.

KIA—Killed In Action. (Since the U.S. was not engaged in a declared war, the use of the term KIA was not authorized. KIA came to mean enemy dead. Americans were KHA or Killed in Hostile Action.)

KLICK—A thousand meters. A kilometer.

LIMA LIMA—Land Line. Refers to telephone communications between two points on the ground.

LLDB—Luc Luong Dac Biet. The South Vietnamese Special Forces. Sometimes referred to as the Look Long, Duck Back.

LP—Listening Post. A position outside the perimeter manned by a couple of soldiers to give advance warning of enemy activity.

LZ—Landing Zone.

M-14—Standard rifle of the U.S., eventually replaced by the M-16. It fires the standard NATO round—7.62 mm.

M-16—Standard infantry weapon of the Vietnam War. It fires 5.56 mm ammunition.

M-79—A short-barrel, shoulder-fired weapon that fires a 40 mm grenade. These can be high explosives, white phosphorus or canister.

MACV—Military Assistance Command, Vietnam, replaced MAAG in 1964.

MEDEVAC—Also called Dustoff. Helicopter used to take the wounded to the medical facilities.

MIA—Missing In Action.

NCO—A Noncommissioned Officer. A noncom. A sergeant.

NCOIC—NCO in charge. The senior NCO in a unit, detachment or patrol.

NEXT—The man who says he is the next to be rotated home. See Short.

NINETEEN—The average age of the combat soldier in Vietnam, as opposed to twenty-six in World War II.

NVA—The North Vietnamese Army. Also used to designate a soldier from North Vietnam.

P (PIASTER)—The basic monetary unit in South Vietnam, worth slightly less than a penny.

PETA-PRIME—A black tarlike substance that melts in the heat of the day to become a sticky, black nightmare that clings to boots, clothes and equipment. It was used to hold down the dust during the dry season.

PETER PILOT—The copilot in a helicopter.

PLF—Parachute Landing Fall. The roll used by parachutists on landing.

POW—Prisoner Of War.

PRC-10—Portable radio. Sometimes called Prick-10.

PRC-25—A lighter portable radio that replaced the PRC-10.

PULL PITCH—Term used by helicopter pilots that means they are going to take off.

PUNJI STAKE—Sharpened bamboo hidden to penetrate the foot, sometimes dipped in feces.

RON—Remain Overnight. Term used by flight crews to indicate a flight that would last longer than a day.

RPD—Soviet light machine gun 7.62 mm.

RTO—Radio Telephone Operator. The radio man of a unit.

SA-2—A surface-to-air missile fired from a fixed site. It is a radar-guided missile that is nearly 35 feet long.

SA-7—A surface-to-air missile that is shoulder-fired and infrared-homing.

SAFE AREA—A Selected Area for Evasion. It doesn't mean that the area is safe from the enemy, only that the terrain, location, or local population make the area a good place for escape and evasion.

SAM TWO—A reference to the SA-2 Guideline.

SAR—Search And Rescue. SAR forces are the people involved in search and rescue missions.

SIX—Radio call sign for the Unit Commander.

SHIT HOOK—Name applied by the troops to the Chinook helicopter because of all the ''shit'' stirred up by its massive rotors.

SHORT—Term used by everyone in Vietnam to tell all who would listen that his tour is about over.

SHORT-TIMER—Person who has been in Vietnam for nearly a year and who will be rotated back to the World soon. When the DEROS (Date of Estimated

Return from Overseas) is the shortest in the unit, the person is said to be "Next."

SKS—Soviet-made carbine.

SMG—Submachine gun.

SOI—Signal Operating Instructions. The booklet that contains the call signs and radio frequencies of the units in Vietnam.

SOP—Standard Operating Procedure.

STEEL POT—The standard U.S. Army helmet. The steel pot is the outer metal cover.

TEAM UNIFORM OR COMPANY UNIFORM—UHF radio frequency on which the team or the company communicates. Frequencies were changed periodically in an attempt to confuse the enemy.

THREE—Radio call sign of the Operations Officer.

THREE CORPS—The military area around Saigon. Vietnam was divided into four corps areas.

TRIPLE A—Antiaircraft Artillery or AAA. This is anything used to shoot at airplanes and helicopters.

THE WORLD—The United States.

TOC—Tactical Operations Center.

TOT—Time Over Target. The time the aircraft are supposed to be over the drop zone with the parachutists, or the target if the planes are bombers.

TWO—Radio call sign of the Intelligence Officer.

TWO-OH-ONE (201) FILE—The military records file that lists a soldier's qualifications, training, experience and abilities.

UMZ—Ultramilitarized Zone. The name GIs gave to the DMZ (Demilitarized Zone).

VC—Vietcong, called Victor Charlie (phonetic alphabet) or just Charlie.

VDI—Vertical Display Indicator. A modern term for the old artificial horizon gauge on the instrument cluster in an aircraft's cockpit.

VIETCONG—A contraction of Vietnam Cong San (Vietnamese Communist).

VIETCONG SAN—The Vietnamese Communists. A term in use since 1956.

WHITE MICE—Refers to the Vietnamese military police because they wore white helmets.

WIA—Wounded In Action.

WILLIE PETE—WP, white phosphorus, called smoke rounds. Also used as antipersonnel weapons.

WINGMAN—Pilot whose job it is to protect another from surprise attack. The number 2 aircraft in an element of two aircraft.

WSO—Weapons System Officer. The name given to the man who rides in the back seat of a Phantom because he is responsible for the weapons systems.

XO—Executive officer of a unit.

YARDS—Short form for Montagnards (pronounced mon-tan-yards).

ZAP—To ding, pop caps, or shoot. To kill.

ZIPPO—A flamethrower.

DON PENDLETON'S EXECUTIONER

MACK BOLAN™

Baptized in the fire and blood of Vietnam, Mack Bolan has become America's supreme hero. Fiercely patriotic and compassionate, he's a man with a high moral code whose sense of right and wrong sometimes violates society's rules. In adventures filled with heart-stopping action, Bolan has thrilled readers around the world. Experience the high-voltage charge as Bolan rallies to the call of his own conscience in daring exploits that place him in peril with virtually every heartbeat.

"Anyone who stands against the civilized forces of truth and justice will sooner or later have to face the piercing blue eyes and cold Beretta steel of Mack Bolan . . . civilization's avenging angel."
— *San Francisco Examiner*

GOLD EAGLE

MB-2R

**Nile Barrabas and the
Soldiers of Barrabas are the**

SOBs

by Jack Hild

Nile Barrabas is a nervy son of a bitch who
was the last American soldier out of Vietnam
and the first man into a new kind of action. His
warriors, called the Soldiers of Barrabas, have
one very simple ambition: to do what the
Marines can't or won't do. Join the Barrabas
blitz! Each book hits new heights—this is
brawling at its best!

"Nile Barrabas is one tough SOB himself. . . .
A wealth of detail. . . . SOBs does the job!"
—*West Coast Review of Books*

**GOLD
EAGLE**

Available wherever paperbacks are sold.

SOBs-1

Mack Bolan's

PHOENIX FORCE

by Gar Wilson

The battle-hardened, five-man commando unit known as
Phoenix Force continues its onslaught against the hard
realities of global terrorism in an endless crusade for
freedom, justice and the rights of the individual. Schooled
in guerrilla warfare, equipped with the latest in lethal
weapons, Phoenix Force's adventures have made them a
legend in their own time. Phoenix Force is the free world's
foreign legion!

**"Gar Wilson is excellent! Raw action attacks
the reader on every page."**

—Don Pendleton

Phoenix Force titles are available
wherever paperbacks are sold.   PF-1

Take
4 explosive books
plus a
mystery bonus
FREE